I0822192

The Last Slinger of Roche

R. M. RHODES

THE LAST SLINGER OF ROCHE

THE CHRONICLES *of* AMARANTHA 1

THE LAST SLINGER OF ROCHE

This book is a work of fiction. Names, characters, places, and incidents are the product of the author's imagination or are used fictitiously. Any resemblance to actual events, locales, or persons, living or dead, is coincidental.

Copyright © 2021 by R.M. Rhodes

All rights reserved.

The scanning, uploading, and distribution of this book without permission is a theft of the author's intellectual property. If you would like permission to use material from the book (other than for review purposes), please contact author.rmrhodes@gmail.com

Cover Design: Enchanted Ink Publishing
Editing: Enchanted Ink Publishing
Formatting: Enchanted Ink Publishing

Ebook ISBN: 979-8-9854393-0-4
Paperback ISBN: 979-8-9854393-1-1
Hardcover ISBN: 979-8-9854393-2-8

Thank you for your support of the author's rights.

Printed in the United States of America

RMRhodes.com

CHAPTER 1

PREAMBLE

I am called many things, but most know me from folktales. My name is Amarantha. Five hundred years' worth of my adventures have either been exaggerated or the details lost from ear to ear. The gods do not allow my stories to be written down, but maybe now is the time to do it myself.

I have come to find that people need stories, fantastical little lies that help us cope or process the events around us. I think that is why there are so many folktales about me. Almost as important as stories, though, is the truth—even if it shatters the little lies we tell ourselves. If you have ever been pulled out of a dream by a slap across the face, then

I think you can relate. Maybe that is just me; I am no good with metaphors. But my point is that I aim to tell the truth no matter the pain it may cause. My interpretation of the world may not align with most people's understanding, but perhaps if I focus on the Unkubernan in this first entry, then the people will see where I am coming from.

The slap that woke me up came from a man of good intentions named Denali, and he showed me the possibilities of a world I could never have imagined on my own. Five hundred years later I am still answering that call to adventure, but now the world watches me. I am Amarantha, adopted daughter of the goddess Ukaleq, shaman of the people, slayer of immortals, skin walker, chaotic. Before I was all these things and more, I was a slinger in the godless wastelands known as the Unkubernan. I was a young woman trained in martial law by the now fallen noble order of Roche. I was a keeper of the peace for the small town of Roca. It was a job I did not want, and a fair majority of the people did not want me, but it was as remote from civilization as possible.

After five hundred years, my life has had many beginnings. This entry is just one of those beginnings. It is not of my youth, not of my training as a slinger in Roche, nor my time crusading in the Unkubernan, but it is my beginning steps toward becoming a chaotic. It is when the idea and possibilities of the outside world opened up to me.

-AMARANTHA

CHAPTER 2

RESPONSIBILITIES

I first met Denali on a day that bears no distinction. Every day in the Unkubernan, no matter the time of year, is the hottest day you can remember. As the local slinger, I was always on duty. It was my charge to be ready at the drop of a hat whenever pilgrims or a challenging slinger made their way into town.

"Get up, Slinger. You're needed," the chief said with a tap of his boot to my bare ass. I slapped my hand down to where he'd kicked me and felt a sheet, so maybe I was not fully bared.

My mind was foggy. I left my head buried in my pillow as it throbbed, my eyes clamped shut.

"You'd better not be hungover again. We've got ourselves a wagon on the horizon."

The fog cleared, and I pushed myself up with a groan. My heart began to race, but my head pounded even harder. The chief had to duck under the rafters. His broad shoulders and plump gut made the entire room look like a child's playroom in comparison.

"Reapers take me," I mumbled as I worked some saliva into my mouth and blinked my eyes open. "How long, Chief?"

"You've got a moment to collect yourself. I'll be downstairs waiting. And Amarantha." He paused from kicking bottles and clothes from his path to point a finger at me. "Don't embarrass us."

I went to speak and found a dry cough in my throat before managing my familiar retort. "Don't tell me how to do my job."

The old man pursed his lips as though something sour had just fallen into his mouth and then caught himself on a set of drawers from tripping over a bottle. "I don't know why that oath of yours couldn't include cleanliness." He huffed in frustration. "Just be ready for negotiations."

The chief ripped open my makeshift curtains to allow the early morning sun to spill into my sorrowful room. The light quickly outshined the dim of my glow stone hanging from the ceiling. No decor or memories adorned the wood panel walls. The room was nothing but an empty set of drawers and a mattress on the floor. My empty bottles littered the matching wood floor. I rubbed my eyes clear to protect from the light and heard the glass from the windowpane crunch under the chief's boot.

"Another broken window? How did you—no, never mind. You do realize the entire building boils in the heat if all the cool air escapes from your window?" He twirled his finger in the direction of the basement. "Those geothermal vents are thousands of years old. I can't repair them if you overwork them. It's not an endless breeze that blows up. The vents only recycle the air."

"I don't think that's how they work," I said.

The chief let out an odd sound between a tsk and a huff. "I'll get Dalek in here to fashion another, but it's coming out of your drinking coin this time." He looked around the room and assessed the current state. "Dayani will be wanting her bottles back. If this wagon is carrying any art or a rug, then you'd best take it. You've been here three years, Amarantha. It's time to move in or move on. I realize you've been through a lot, but you can't keep going like this. You need—"

I cut him off with a wave of my hand, and he pursed his lips again. The old man would lecture any chance he got. I could not for the life of me remember breaking the window, but that was the least of my concerns as my aching mind began to process the time.

"Did they travel through the night?" I asked.

"If they did, they must have a powerful slinger accompanying them to survive the predators—maybe one of your old buddies from Roche."

With a nasty grin that implied the threat of a former Roche slinger, the chief left the room for me to wash up and put some clothes on. I moved to stand and found my limbs so stiff that I fell right back onto the mattress. The springs let out a squeaky moan under my weight. My vision blurred slightly as the blood rushed to my head. As it cleared, I noticed a darkness in the corner of my eye. I blinked and rolled my eyes to see if it would clear, but the dark mass was not in my vision. It sat in the corner of the room.

I quickly reached for the necklace with a red stone pendant that lay on the floor near my bed and recited part of my oaths.

"My jurisdiction is the Unkubernan. My authority is my covenant. My duty is my people." When I opened my eyes, the dark mass that had sat in the corner of my room was gone.

"Reapers take—" I cut off the curse before I could finish.

I took a deep breath. This was the fifth time in as many days. Either I was going mad or . . . I looked down to Death's stone in my hand. No, the alternative was far too frightening. I reached for last night's bottle and was rewarded with a few drops to clear my palate. I tossed the bottle into a corner pile of similar bottles. The chief was right, of course. Dayani did not like it when I took the bottles home from the tavern, but there was no other way to cure the boredom out here. I would need to get the empty bottles back to her at some point or she would likely cut me off, and that absolutely could not happen. Boredom led to questioning how I'd gotten stuck out here in the first place. There were only two cures for boredom in the Unkubernan: a stiff drink or a good tussle with a fine man. Fine men were not easy to find this far out, so the drink became my best friend.

None of my clothes had been laundered in weeks. I had been wearing the cleanest shirt for three days now, and it was still damp with sweat from the day before. It was a good fit but clung to my already sweaty skin. The trousers were covered in dust, and there was no time to beat them clean. The boots were my favorite. I had bought them off a caravan that had lost their slinger to the beasts of the night. I considered the discount they'd given me to be a fine donation for my protection.

I made for the door but paused to slap my hip and realized my munition was missing. My eyes surveyed the room for my handcrafted slinger totems. The tiny black orbs, which were no larger than a fingernail, were nowhere to be seen.

There should have been at least the six I'd carried on me the night before. I only wore the traditional six when confronting potential duelists. I reached out with my mind and felt my connection to them. Like a string on the end of my fingertip, I tugged at that connection and was rewarded with all six orbs zipping toward me from under my bed. I caught the totems and slapped three to my hip and three to the small of my back, where that same stringlike connection coiled tight and held them in place.

Before I could close the door behind me, I caught the faint sound of squeaky wagon wheels crunching dirt clods and bumping over rocks. To my ears this meant the wagon had not yet breached Main Street. If it had, the echo would've likely rattled these old buildings.

Upon exiting my room, I peered over the banister to the chief's hall below and saw the crowd of elders convening around the long table. The chief's wife struggled to maintain a semblance of order as the group presented different needs of the town they felt should be prioritized in negotiations. One voice boomed over the others. There was a sense of urgency in his tone.

"Change is coming, I tell you! I got word the last time I was in Takan that some gangs are large enough to take over whole towns now. It doesn't matter how many shots live in the city."

Another elderly voice broke out over the crowd. "Even if that's true, Carr, we're far enough out that no one pays us any mind unless they're foreign pilgrims looking for the goddess." The crowd murmured agreement. "It's the demigods we need to be worried about." The murmured agreement turned to groans. "There have been more sightings. They all saw the same thing as me. The great white serpent has been spotted. Without the slingers of Roche, the dangers of the Unkubernan are growing!"

Voices clamored over the two bickering men in their own urgent responses, and I paid them no mind. That same elder had been warning about gangs since the order of Roche fell three years ago.

I noticed two female elders at the bottom of the stairs as I descended. They stood apart from the group jockeying to be heard and instead appeared to be gossiping. They were old enough that nothing they said was a whisper.

"I just don't understand why she's still staying in Chieftain Hall. Shouldn't she take quarter above the jailhouse?"

I froze on the stairs when I realized they were speaking of me.

"In Vertere's old quarters?" the other woman responded, aghast. "Why should she?"

The first woman shrugged. "She's the town's slinger. It makes more sense than inconveniencing the chief and his wife."

"Oh, Kamil," the second woman began in a condescending tone. "She may have beaten Vertere in their duel, allegedly, but she isn't one of us. She's an outsider. She doesn't care about us, and she doesn't have this town's best interest at heart. Sure, she defends her post from other challengers, but she's not a keeper of the peace. She's got no plans to account for the changes in the Unkubernan."

"All I'm saying is she's been here three years now, and she was a slinger of Roche, for god's sake. She's young. Maybe we're expecting too much."

"*Was* and *is* are very different, Kamil, and we're not expecting much from the girl. She needs to get her head out of her ass. As capable as she may be as a slinger, we don't need a broken thing this far out in the Unkubernan. We need a pillar for the community, like Vertere was. We need solutions to our problems."

I began descending the stairs again. The jolt of being the topic of gossip had worn off, and I had places to be. Broken or not, these old women could not see the value in the safety I guaranteed the town.

"What we don't need"—both women jumped and turned to see me standing over them—"is more old bureaucrats who argue all day and can't pull their own weight around here. You know what we did with slingers in Roche who managed to survive until they got old?" The women did not respond. "We sent them on a foolish pilgrimage to the goddess Ukaleq. Would you two like to take the pilgrimage?"

The women shook their heads, and Kamil spoke up. "Beg your pardon, Amarantha. We didn't mean any offense. You know how old women get." She smiled weakly.

I did not like the way they were looking at me. They were scared. I'd spent three years protecting this town from beasts and gangs and errant slingers, and they still looked at me as a wild thing. Apparently, all that effort meant nothing to them if they did not like me or trust me. A slinger of Roche without the leash of their covenant was a wild animal to these people. I smiled.

"Oddly enough, the crusades didn't prepare me for small-town life. Gossip away and forgive my youth, though I'd wager I've seen more of the Unkubernan than this whole town put together. I'll be here looking after the town long after you two are gone. Now if you'll excuse me, broken or not, I need to go do my job—the part of my job that keeps you all safe and keeps our economy functioning. But please, don't let me interfere with the important bureaucracy of the council of elders." I gestured to the group of old men and women lobbying to be heard.

The women nodded and stepped apart, allowing me to pass.

"She's sassier than the whole town combined too," the old woman quipped to her friend louder than she probably realized. Kamil shushed her.

CHAPTER 3

SLINGERS

I left the hall and stepped out into the heat of the sun. I squinted reflexively, and the pounding in my head stopped for the briefest moment, but it came back even fiercer than before. I took a sharp breath through my nose and felt the heat mixed with the smell of dirt. It was not so hot that it burned, but it would not be long before the heat would dry out my sinuses until they cracked. The chief was waiting in the middle of the road, the bald spot on the top of his head shining with the rising sun as he applied balm to his lips and cheeks. He had his three totems clipped into a belt at his waist. Most of the townsfolk were on their porches waiting to see how they might benefit from negotiations. The elders began to file out behind me, led by Kamil and the bitter old woman she had been gossiping with. I turned my attention back to the chief.

"You've got a new totem," I said, pointing to the third orb on his belt.

"I've not finished making the orb my totem yet, but I might sling it with the force of a fist in a pinch," he said.

"Ah, well it's a good thing you won't need it then. Best just to leave it for show."

He nodded and adjusted the belt on his waist where the orbs sat in their clips. He did not have the skill to coil them in place, but he had more orbs on his belt than most.

I looked out to the approaching wagon. It had come from the southern plateaus, the normal route from some of the larger cities in the Unkubernan. The two creatures pulling the wagon were new to me; they were not the muscular beasts I was used to seeing. Their bodies were just layer upon layer of round shells coalescing upon one another, and each had eight or more legs that looked like sticks, no muscle to them at all. The only feature that distinguished their heads was the two long antennae that protruded from the blunt end of the coalescing shells. They looked more like something I would find scuttling away if I flipped over a large stone. They looked like one of Death's insects, not a creature of one of the great spirits.

There was a man walking beside the wagon. He was even younger than me. He could not have been older than twenty, and he looked soft. The orbs that glistened on his hip meant he was a slinger even if his wide-brimmed hat sat like an oversize bucket on his head. There was no way this boy had delivered them through the desert at night. Every caravan needed at least one slinger to survive the wilderness, but traveling at night took an extra level of experience.

"That's far enough!" I called out to the coach driver.

He pulled on the reins and brought the wagon to a halt. The two creatures curled up and rolled over almost immediately. They were stopped in front of the town jail, Vertere's old place. The former slinger's massive boulder of a totem still lay in front of the building like a stubborn reminder of his importance to the people here. Even if the people had been willing to move the boulder, it was doubtful the concentrated efforts of the town could make it budge.

The chief furrowed his brow at me and walked closer to the wagon. I followed close behind and took the opportunity to feel out some of the totems I'd left strewn about town. Of course they were there, but reaching out and feeling them one by one had become a game of sorts in my mind, instinctual even.

"Hail, travelers! Welcome to Roca!" he called to them.

I winced as the yell pounded in my head but tried not to let my irritation show. The coach driver pulled back his hood, revealing a blunt yet distinguished face, and smiled. Smiles were dangerous. The man's cloak was ornate. It hardly carried any dust on it and had a sheen from a type of fiber I did not recognize. On most of his fingers he wore one type of ring or another, but a few of his fingers looked as though they had been broken before. He had a few scars on the parts of his arms that peeked through his brilliant cloak. Even from a few paces away it was obvious his hands had seen decades of labor, and yet with all his adornment, standing next to the young slinger, the coach driver looked like a king. A tradesman turned king, but a king nonetheless. All pilgrims were foreigners to the Unkubernan, and they came in all different shapes and tones, but he looked more foreign than most. He looked rich enough to afford a better slinger than this kid, or at least more of them.

"Good day to you, Chief." He turned in his coach box to look at me. "An honor, young slinger." His voice was hoarse, but the melody of his baritone was soothing.

The boyish slinger stepped forward. "That's their slinger? Why are we wasting our time? She's not a threat."

I couldn't stop the corner of my mouth from briefly letting a smirk peek through.

"Peace, young Yuma." All the melody dropped from his tone when he spoke to the young slinger, like a father explaining something for the hundredth time to a child. "Forgive my young friend here. It's been a long journey, and he gets moody quite easily."

Yuma's face was all scowl as he continued to size me up.

"How long will you be staying?" The chief was projecting from his diaphragm loud enough for the whole town to hear. I took a few steps to the side for the sake of my head. "And what services are you in need of, Master . . . ?" The chief trailed off, waiting for an introduction.

"Denali, if you will. But before we begin negotiations, I have a sensitive matter to discuss with you privately, Chief."

I shifted my weight, leaning out my hip to relax, and crossed my arms. "How many slingers are you hiding in the wagon?" I said.

Yuma immediately readied his stance, prepared to draw an orb, but I ignored him.

Denali looked to me apologetically and flourished a slight bow. "That would be the sensitive matter."

The chief's face turned red. With a quick glance, I could not tell if he was angry or just petrified. Either way, he was pursing his lips again, looking like he might pop.

"You do not seem too worried," Denali said as he leaned forward with another of those dangerous smiles.

I kept my arms crossed and my hip out as I looked him straight in the eye. "I'm not."

"What if I told you I had ten slingers?" he said.

The melody in his baritone sounded amused. I shrugged.

"Do you know who I am?" came an indignant voice from the left.

I kept my eyes trained on Denali and his smile as I twitched my finger under my arm, a gesture no one else would see. One of my orbs that was strewn about the town flew toward me. It zipped through the top of Yuma's hat, piercing a hole and knocking it off his head. The orb arced down into the palm of my hand, still under crossed arms. Denali's smile broadened. I kept my stare trained on him without expression. Something about this pilgrim did not add up to me—too many contradictions.

"How dare you!" Yuma screamed, but Denali waved him off and interrupted the young man's tirade.

"Peace, Yuma. She has you beat, and I did not want a fight in the first place. Keep your mouth shut if you want full payment." He finally let go of his gaze on me and turned to the chief. "I apologize for the deception, Chief.

It was not my wish to provoke a fight. I am more than willing, and able as you can imagine, to pay for services. We only need to stay a few days until the rest of our party joins us."

The young Yuma was fuming now, poking at the new hole in his wide-brimmed hat.

"This is quite unorthodox, Denali." The chief was clearly still flustered.

"More slingers in the party you're waiting on?" I prodded.

Denali turned to me and let out a troubled sigh. "Just one more. I am a pilgrim passing through the Unkubernan to receive the goddess Ukaleq's blessing."

The rest of the slingers exited the wagon: one woman with a nasty scar down her cheek and two burly men, possibly brothers. Their true features were hard to make out through their beards.

I let out a sigh and uncrossed my arms to show that I was not hiding any movements before continuing to address them all.

"Well, if you can afford all these slingers, then I say you're most welcome here."

The four slingers were all glaring at me now. Despite their seniority, they stood behind Yuma as though he was in charge. He did not seem all that dangerous, though.

"What gang are you all with?" I asked.

Yuma's overconfident smile confirmed my suspicions, but the others shifted uneasily.

"Gang?" Denali asked as he turned the question to the group of slingers behind him.

If the man did not know he had employed a gang then maybe his smiles were genuine. I felt a little heat in my chest thinking about the distraction of exploring his contradictions for the next few days.

"No matter." I brushed Denali and the gang off with a curt wave. "Denali, you are welcome to stay at the tavern, or you can find me at Chieftain Hall," I added with a wink. The red in his cheeks was a curious response. Most pilgrims I propositioned simply put on a goofy grin. "The rest of you slingers, listen up. My name is Amarantha. You will stay outside of town after dark. There is a small furnished cabin to the north that will accommodate you. If you are seen in town after dark, I will not hesitate to put you down. If you wish to challenge me to be the slinger of this town, please coordinate with the chief, and we'll have a fair duel as tradition dictates."

Yuma spat a yellow paste from his cheek onto the ground and grinned. "You think you're some kind of Roche slinger or something? Or are we so far out you all haven't caught up with the times?"

The chief stepped forward this time. "Listen here, you man-child. Amarantha here was—"

I released the tension of a coiled orb and directed it into the sky. A sudden crack rang through the air, cutting off the chief. He knew better than to talk about my past for me, especially to strangers. The four slingers were ready to draw, each with an orb floating off their belts. I kept my arms folded as Denali jumped off the wagon and landed between me and his hired help.

The four slingers' expressions were growing much darker, but they relaxed at Denali's behest.

"What I am," I said, looking to each of the slingers, "is this town's authority. Consider yourselves lucky that I am willing to fight fair if need be."

"I think you've played your cards, girl," Yuma said.

"Maybe I have. Maybe these six shots at my hip are all I have left, or maybe you're standing in my trap, young Yuma." I knew better than to antagonize, but his growl made it worth it. "Maybe I have hundreds of orbs ready to skewer you if you so much as step out of line. Give me a reason," I sneered.

"I know you're bluffing now, and you definitely ain't no Roche slinger if you've got more than six."

I leveled a glare at him. "Careful."

His grin turned wicked. His eyes twitched, barely masking his longing for bloodshed. He widened his stance slightly, and his breathing grew deeper. Denali stepped in front of him, and Yuma's eyes went wide and bulged as they slowly turned to look at him.

I could not see Denali's face, but I saw that his staff touched Yuma's chest. "Do not make me repeat myself, Yuma." The man's melodic baritone was nothing more than a low rumble now.

Yuma pulled back from Denali's staff and crossed his arms as he turned away from Denali, excusing himself from the rest of the conversation. Before Denali could turn back to me and the chief, the woman with the scar running down her face spoke up.

"Are you the same Amarantha that Slalal took in?"

I felt my heart catch in my throat at my mentor's name but did my best not to let any expression show on my face. I nodded.

"We need to leave," the woman said to Denali.

Denali turned back to me and looked between us.

"Do you know each other, Tokala?" he asked.

"No, but I know of her." Yuma's ears perked up from

his pouting, and he looked me over as Tokala reasoned with Denali. "She could kill us all. She was trained by the grand master of the Roche slingers."

"Very interesting," Denali said with an unwavering stare. "I gathered there were not any slingers of Roche left."

"There aren't," she continued. "Nobody has the oaths, and most were hunted down after their order fell apart. She has no reason to keep her word."

"Amarantha has been our slinger for three years, and not once has she broken her word. I have officiated every duel," the chief said.

One of the bearded men scoffed as he turned to the other. "Could be a crooked chief for all we know."

"You dare question the honor of our town?"

I put a hand on the chief's arm and watched the fire in his eyes simmer.

"That is enough of that." Denali snapped his fingers to call everyone's eyes and pointed to the two burly men who stood back with Yuma. "We do not negotiate passage by insulting an entire town. I intend to play by the rules. You all being members of a gang changes nothing. It's my pocketbook funding this, remember?"

Denali walked over to me, never breaking eye contact, and reached out a hand. I reached forward and met his calloused grip.

"What say you?" he asked. "Do you intend to kill us as Tokala claims you are able to do?"

"I say what I already said." I met his hard studying gaze. "You all are welcome here so long as you don't cause trouble. Step out of line and I won't hesitate to put you down before you can draw an orb. If anyone wants a duel, I accept your challenge, and it will be a fair fight." Still holding his hand firmly, I looked past Denali to the small gang of slingers and addressed them directly. "But if you've never fought in a real duel with a Roche slinger, then fair warning, you don't stand a chance."

Movement in the distance caught my eye. I looked past the slingers and past the edge of town toward the plateaus they'd come from. A large white mass slithered behind the plateau. *Reapers,* I thought. *That was big.* Had I just witnessed the demigod the old man had been on about? My eyes dropped back down to the situation at hand. The slingers stood quietly. I looked to Denali. He still stared into my eyes, hands clasped. I looked over to the chief, but he was focused on Denali. Nobody had seen it. Denali's expression softened, and I shook my head free from what I had just witnessed.

"Well, that is good enough for me." He smiled and turned to Tokala but spoke loud enough for the whole town. "This woman's honest word is worth following to the end of the world and back."

"What is that supposed to mean? How do you divine something like that?" the chief asked.

"Just an old shaman trick," Denali said.

I raised an eyebrow. "Sounds invasive."

Denali's only response was an apologetic bow.

The chief let out a long breath, and I rubbed my forehead to combat the throbbing before continuing my instruction.

"Well, if there are no more questions, the tavern is just there." I pointed behind them. "Treat Dayani nice, and her husband will treat you to any melody you can imagine." I pointed back over my shoulder. "Winona's is that way if you need your clothes laundered or a bath. Tab's over there is the general store. The chief here will negotiate prices with you. Chief, I'll need a word with you later." I began to turn and caught a glimpse of the old godless shaman glaring at me from his storefront. "Oh, and our local shaman, Tali, is next door to the tavern, but he's shit since there are no gods in the Unkubernan, so don't let the chief take too much of your money if you need that man's services. In fact, if you're a shaman, Denali, the town could likely use your services for barter. We have stones that lost their glow, and some of the soil could use a blessing." I continued walking backward toward Chieftain Hall. "And my room is this way."

I added that last bit to see if his cheeks would turn red again, and they did. The chief began negotiations, and I turned to see a few of the elders glaring at me from their porches. My head was aching too much to find out what I had done wrong this time.

"I can assure you Tali is one of the finest. He's actually an invoker, believe it or not."

I heard the chief's voice trailing off as I made my way back to my room to grab my laundry. My own smell was beginning to distract me, and there was a good chance for company tonight.

CHAPTER 4

INVOKE

I dropped a bag full of clothes off to Winona and found myself with two young boys tailing me at a distance. They had emerged from Winona's laundry and bathhouse, leaving me to assume they were hers. I did not appreciate the entourage. I stopped abruptly and turned back in a swift motion, making them jump back.

"What do you want?"

The two boys fidgeted. "Ask her," the younger one prodded.

The older boy mustered his courage and stepped forward. He held forth a small rock he must have plucked from the ground. "Can you teach us to be slingers?"

The boy looked to be a few inches from puberty, but he was larger than I'd been when I found myself orphaned in the wilderness.

"Go ask the chief. If he says you aren't old enough, tell him I said it was fine. I don't have time for kids."

"We don't want him to teach us. He taught the others. Only a Roche slinger could scare a gang, and they said the grand master taught you. Is that true?"

I looked between the boys. "You Winona's kids?"

The older boy nodded. "I am Yelm, son of Dalek. This is my younger brother, Nisqually . . . also son of Dalek."

I smirked. "Thanks for the clarification. Dalek the master carpenter? I didn't realize he and Winona were married," I mused.

The older boy's grin grew broad at the mention of his father, and he nodded vigorously. The younger boy stepped forward with one of my totems in hand. He clenched the orb and then opened his hand to see if it moved. "I can't work it out."

I let out a deep sigh.

The older boy turned to scold the younger one. "You don't even know the basics. That's her totem. It's worthless to you."

"Totem?" the younger boy asked.

I tugged on my connection to the orb. It whipped out of the younger boy's hand and into my own.

"Everything has a spirit. I tuned the spirit of this orb to my spirit, so now it's my totem. I have authority over it, and it gives me a special connection to it." I flipped the orb over my shoulder into the street. "If you find one of my orbs lying around, you'd best leave it alone. It's a trap. You don't want it in your pocket if I have need of it, or your mom will whip you for a hole in your trousers . . . or your leg."

Both boys stared at me, either attempting to process what I'd said or unable to decide which question in a river of questions was the right question to ask. The younger boy slowly looked to his brother and then back to me with wide fearful eyes.

"I have a spirit. Can you make me into a totem?"

"What?" It took me a moment to process the absurdity. "No, of course not. Physiologically you are much more complex than a rock, so your spirit is more complex too." I turned to look at the older boy. "They teach you to read yet?"

"Yes, ma'am." His eyes snapped forward.

"Ma'am," I scoffed under my breath as I walked over to the bench outside Tab's general store. "Fetch me a paper and lead from Tab. Tell him it's for Amarantha."

The older boy darted inside the storefront. The little one stood in the sun where his brother had left him and stared at me. When the small boy did not break his gaze, I shifted slightly and rubbed my temples to nurse my growing headache. "Get out of the sun," I chided the little one.

The boy took the invitation to sit on the bench next to me, still watching me, but with the corner of his eye and a few hesitant glances. Even with the pounding in my head, the boy's awkwardness made me smile. The older boy ran out of the storefront and thrust the paper and lead in front of me. The little one stood up on the bench to look over my shoulder as I wrote. Unlike his older brother, I was certain he could not read.

My jurisdiction is the Unkubernan
My authority is my covenant
My duty is my people
To uphold justice as truth demands
To protect those that cannot protect themselves
To maintain peace and security
I will only kill when proof of truth warrants
I will take up the mantle of town protector should it fall to me
I will never abuse my power or ask of any

I left out the beginning and end of the covenant, the dangerous bits, and proffered the results to the older boy.

"That right there, boys, is the Slinger's Oath. They taught it to us out in Roche. Taught to me by my mentor."

"The grand master," Yelm said in a reverent whisper.

"Read it over until you have it memorized, then come back when you've found your own orb and have enough authority over it to make it your totem. When you're old enough and have shown you can follow the creed on your own, I will teach you how to fight. Now don't bother me in the morning ever again."

They ran off giggling to the schoolyard, not yet realizing what they were in for. Hopefully I'd just bought myself a few years before they bothered me again. My eyes could not follow them for long before the strain of my headache pulled my eyes shut.

I made up my mind and stood to make my way to Tali's. Despite the advice I had given Denali and his accompanying gang, I needed some medicine from the old quack if I was to make it through the day. I passed the old couple who managed the stables as they worked to figure out how to accommodate the strange creatures that had pulled Denali's wagon into town. I slowed my gait and contemplated helping them. Anything was better than engaging with Tali, and the gossiping old ladies were in my head now. The people here wanted more from their slinger than protection; they wanted a leader, a local. But the throb in my head kept me moving forward.

"I'll give you a hand after I wrap up an errand," I called to the two, whose names I had never bothered to recall.

"We'll manage," the old man said as he raised a flat palm in my direction without ever looking my way.

The old woman next to him spared me a few glances but never said a word. I now remembered why I had not bothered to learn their names. I shook my head at the stubborn contradiction that was the people of Roca. *They want more from their slinger, but they don't want help from an outsider.* I put my head down and rubbed my forehead as I approached Tali's. The sign out front had a fresh coat of paint. I had never been able to make it out before, but now it clearly read "Tali's, Invoker for Body, Mind, and Soul."

I took a deep breath and hesitated before opening the door, knowing full well how he would greet me and the den of elders he would have to back up his acrid personality.

"Can't squint through a duel," I muttered to myself and pushed the door open.

I stepped into the thick wall of smoke that always permeated the storefront. As I fanned away the smoke from my already dry eyes, I was relieved to see only two of the elders lounging in the storefront. Tali was behind the counter puffing into his pipe when he looked up to see me.

"Well, if it isn't the great pretender. Look, boys, it's the last true slinger of Roche."

They didn't look up from their pipes or their game as Tali laughed.

"Cut the pleasantries, you old shit-fire. I need something for my head."

"Respect your elders, girl. I heard what you said to the pilgrim about my business. I'll have you know, they held the chief to it. I'm gonna have to charge you extra for the medicine today, and you get the bitter one."

"If you were a real shaman you wouldn't need a storefront full of all this." I gestured to the shelves of bottled roots and thistles hanging from the beams.

"I don't claim to be a shaman; they've ruined the term. I'm an invoker. Shamans are supposed to be about living with nature, not manipulating it." He spat onto the floorboards. "I won't have none of it in my store."

I couldn't stop my eyes from rolling. "Is that what all this invoker business on the sign out front is about?"

The old man lifted his chin in the air. "An invoker is what I am. It's more than a vocation; it's a way of life. A real slinger would understand. Vertere understood. He only carried six orbs on his belt, like a true slinger of Roche. He probably rolls in his grave every time you make a new one."

I shook my head. "I grew up in Roche, and I've crusaded across the Unkubernan from one provincial town to the next. Nobody ever talked about an invoker. Hell, I've been here three years, and all I've ever seen you do is sell herbs and oils and smoke yourself into a stupor."

One of the elders took a moment from his game to chuckle. "She's got you there, Tali," he said without looking over.

"I'm grieving, and I also happen to be an herbalist," Tali said.

The other elder leaned forward and gave his companion an open-palmed tap on the side of his head. "You know how close he was to Vertere."

The word *invoker* had been rolling through my mind during their exchange. "If you are not a shaman, how is an invoker different? Invoke sounds like you call on the power of gods. That's what shamans do."

Tali waved his pipe and set it down on the counter. "Shamans these days are all about authority over nature. They shape the world around them through the authority of their great spirit or their own personal authority. It's unnatural." He picked up his pipe again and drew a long breath. "Invokers keep the balance of nature through hymns. We communicate with gods in the spiritual realm. We find ailments in the spirits of our brothers and restore them."

Tali took another long drag of his pipe and let the smoke spew into a cloud between us.

"There are no gods in the Unkubernan," I said. "They left, and they aren't welcome back."

"Who's going to see to that?" he asked. "There is no authority left in the Unkubernan. The slingers of Roche are no more. Their covenant is shattered, and the city is gone. Nothing but craters left. I suppose you could go back to crusading if you wanted." He chuckled to himself but looked to the other two elders to see if they would laugh. They did not.

"The demigods," I said in realization. "Are the gods pushing back into our borders? The white serpent."

Tali's eyes lit up. "Did you spot that one near town?

Interesting. You don't need to worry about him. In fact, you don't need to worry about gods coming into the Unkubernan. Not this deep at least. The great spirits have no need of the Unkubernan. They forsook their duties and abandoned us for the coast millennia ago. Now if you want this medicine for your head, then pay up. I'm done humoring the likes of you. It's double today."

"No one else in town charges me." I immediately regretted giving him more to complain about.

"I know better." The old man pointed his pipe at me. "They fear you, and I don't. I see you for what you are."

"Looked at my spirit, did you?"

"He couldn't if he wanted to," the more talkative of the two elders said. "He's been too high on the pops since you killed Vertere."

"Hush, you," Tali snapped. "I don't need to see your spirit to know you're a charlatan girl pretending to live up to Roche covenants."

"What's wrong with living up to a covenant?" I asked.

"You don't get to come into our town and kill our slinger of Roche and then take up his mantle while pretending to be better than him. To spit on his memory. These people deserve better than you."

"I protect them."

"Are you demanding free services, Slinger?" The old man spread his legs out from the perch on his stool and bit his cheek as he stared me down.

I clenched my fist and looked away only to see the other men looking up to watch the exchange.

"How does it go?" The old invoker began to quote the same oath I had just shared with those boys. "I will never abuse my power or ask of any. Is that it?" The old man had a broad grin now. "So are you demanding, Slinger? It's all right if you do; it'll just prove my point about all your pretending."

"I'm not demanding anything, you old cretin, and whether I choose to follow an oath is none of your concern. If I choose to live up to that oath, then what does it matter to you?"

"There are no more slingers of Roche, girl. Quit pretending. The oath broke for all of them, and you continue on just to feign innocence. You can't pull the wool over my eyes."

"Some of us don't need the threat of death to keep our oaths," I sneered.

"Says the woman who killed Vertere. He was a real slinger of Roche."

The other elders murmured in agreement.

I unclenched my fist and worked my jaw to loosen it as they murmured. "We don't need to get into it today. Just give me the medicine. I'll pay."

"Patience." He scowled. "I wasn't finished. Vertere was the protector of this town for forty years before you came and put an orb through his chest."

I could feel the heat boiling up from my neck into my scalp as my jaw clenched back up. One of the elders spoke up in agreement before I could calm myself down.

"He never said one unkind word. That's not part of their oath."

"He always stopped to help," said the other elder.

"The memorial was three years ago," I said, "and the chief ruled it self-defense. He saw what your supposed hero tried to pull on me. If the chief hadn't, then I wouldn't be stuck here."

"You ain't stuck, girl." Tali was standing now. "You aren't sworn to death no more, no one from Roche is, not that I believe you ever were. Do us all a favor and leave."

I slammed my palm onto the counter between us. "That is up to the chief, not you, you backwater mushroom peddler." I waved a pointed finger in the direction of the two elders. "You old shits need to accept the truth and quit worshiping a man who felt so threatened by a young woman that he'd smile to my face and then try to put an orb through my back."

The elders were standing now. Tali turned and thumped the medicine I so desperately wanted back on the shelf. He turned to me and stepped out from behind the counter. The old man had to look up at me, but his air was intense as he approached.

"Vertere did more good in his life than you ever will. One mistake isn't the sum of a man's life."

The two elders stood behind Tali, defending the memory of their late friend and protector. I stood my ground.

"You seem damn intent on making sure his one mistake defines *my* life!" I yelled back.

I turned on my heel and marched out the door, slamming it behind me.

CHAPTER 5

SHAMAN

I let out a long breath and left the covered porch of Tali's store before anyone could follow me out. In the past, their glares felt like they could chase off a pack of roaming beasts. With the current heat in my cheeks, I could tell I might do something foolish if they tried those looks on me any further.

I walked by the stables, where the old couple had been wrangling the shelled beasts. They appeared to have given up and left the creatures to their own devices in the sun. The creatures were curled up inside their coalescing black shells. They looked like massive stones that had always been a part of the road.

A few paces over, the pilgrim's wagon was parked in front of the alley that lay between the stables and the tavern. Denali was sitting on the back with a long line of townspeople holding their various collections of stones or plants that needed reminding of their jobs. I stood in the shade of the building and watched the exchange for a moment. I needed a distraction to cool off. One person handed Denali a stone that just barely let off a yellow hue. He took it in his hand and studied it for a moment, then the stone lit up brighter than it probably ever had. The next person in line handed him a small withered plant. He took the pot in hand and began whispering to it. The plant stood up straight, the branches grew longer, and it grew another foot in height as little orange balls began to sprout. Denali proceeded to give the townsman instructions for its care.

I juggled one of my totems in my hand as I watched, twirling the orb between my fingers using that string-like connection, my authority over it. It took most people years to develop a totem. I had a knack for it that my mentor had frowned upon. A true slinger of Roche only needed six to master the Noble Forms, but in a land of cheats and crooks, nobility got you killed.

I dropped the orb in my distraction, then tugged on the connection until it flung back up into my palm, never touching the ground. This authority made sense to me. I could feel the connection I had with the totem and tugged at it to control it. I tossed the orb out in front of me to stretch out the connection and quickly pulled to wind it up tight again before slapping it to my hip. The coil allowed me to release the orb at high speed, but what Denali was doing did not make as much sense. These objects he was helping the people with were not his totems; they were not within his god's jurisdiction, yet he had some kind of authority over them, enough to express his will and change their very nature. Gods were said to have limited authority over all things. The greater the god, the greater their natural authority over all living things. I did not know what determined greatness or if Denali's god could really be considered that great. He was different than other shamans who had come through before. Some had lost their favor with their god and had no authority, some were questing and could still express some authority over items like Denali was, but it was more than just the speed in which he helped the people.

Denali took the next glow stone in hand with the same enthusiasm he had shown for every other item before. He spoke with every person and asked questions, before taking a moment to study the object intently and whisper to it then waited for the reaction. Every time he made a stone glow or wilting plant come back to life, it put a new smile on his face.

The man moved through a handful of customers as I stood there watching. The next person offered him coin after their exchange, but Denali refused. Curious, I pushed off the wall and began to walk by to catch the exchange.

"Not necessary. I am happy to help," Denali said.

"But the chief didn't negotiate for these services," the mother with a child on her hip said.

"Where I come from, these services are free. It is no trouble at all."

I kept walking by. Most shamans who came through town used their services to negotiate better prices. This man was either very rich or very stupid.

The sound of music from the tavern caught my attention as I passed. I paused to mull over my options. My head was getting worse, and Dayani and Monte might've been my last recourse at relief. The two of them would occasionally take hikes to find herbs despite my protests. There were a few occasions when I had woken up early and spotted Dayani running into the barren wilderness for a morning jog. Mad as the two were, they were kind and might've had a cure they could spare for my head.

I stopped by my room at Chieftain Hall to grab a few empty bottles so that I could win Dayani's favor. The chief was in the main hall holding council with some of the elders as I slipped back down. The chief's wife was dutifully moderating the voices and counting coins into different piles, most of which looked to be gold.

The chief spotted me slipping by and jumped up to hobble over to me as he worked the blood back into his legs from sitting on the hard stool.

"Amarantha," he called in a hushed tone while flagging me down.

His sour expression from the morning had faded and now looked quite sympathetic. I felt a slight pang of guilt at the squinted furrowed expression I could not wipe from my face.

"You said you wanted to talk. What is it?"

"Turned out to be nothing," I lied.

In the moment, the gargantuan white serpent had felt so real, but I had also been seeing a black mass. There was no need to cause alarm.

"No matter. I wanted to apologize for almost letting slip your"—he looked over his shoulder and hushed his tone further—"past affiliations. Your secret is safe with me. I swear it."

I rubbed my eyebrows to soften the look on my face before looking back up to him. He was a good man trying his hardest, and he did not deserve half the flak I gave him.

"Let's just be clear for the future. The whole town knows my past as an apprentice Roche slinger, but that doesn't mean anyone outside of the town should know it, even if that Tokala lady figured it out. It'll only put us on the map and draw attention."

"Agreed, and again, I'm sorry." He looked truly chastened.

I looked to make sure no one was in earshot before continuing.

"And our absolute secret? Just the two of us? You haven't slipped that at all? Not even talking in your sleep?"

He shook his head furiously and then opened his mouth slightly, working out the words he wanted to say next. "It's your choice, mind you, but it would be easier if the others knew. That your oaths are—" He cut himself off. "They might understand you better is all—especially Tali and some of the elders. It's hard to explain why I let an outsider stay sometimes."

My scowl came back even fiercer than before as I pointed a finger up toward his chest.

"Absolutely not."

His hands went up into the air as casually as he could muster, and he looked around to see if anyone was watching. "I understand. It's your choice. No need to appear threatening."

"Good," I said. "It's one thing if rumors spread to other towns and gangs that a former slinger of Roche is in town. It would be suicide for the whole town if rumor spread that there's a slinger who is still sworn on Death. Don't forget it." I poked him in the sternum and turned to leave the hall.

"Amarantha," the chief called after me. "I know the gang is probably preoccupying you, but keep an eye on Denali as well."

"Why?" I asked. "He seems honest."

"He has been out there helping the people with their stones and such for free. He didn't use it to barter." The chief looked for more words by moving his hands. "It just seems off is all."

I shrugged. "He's a dead man walking, right? Might just be that he's feeling charitable before he marches into the unknown."

I turned back to the door and left.

Every time I stepped out of a building and my eyes adjusted to the sun, it acted as a multiplier to the pain in my head. I marched through the brightness with my eyes mostly closed and covered with my hand as I made my way to the tavern. As expected, the newcomers were already making themselves comfortable, Denali more so than the others. He was cheering on Monte, the local musician, and pestering him for songs the man had never heard of. I was quite surprised to see him already in the tavern drinking. The line of townspeople had been quite long.

The gang of slingers was huddled at the bar discussing something in hushed tones. I made my way past their glances and Yuma's glare to Denali and sat down at his table, letting the small burlap of empty bottles clank to the floor next to me. The man's cheeks were already getting a flush from the alcohol, but his eyes were just as clear and focused as before. His smile came through as warm and endearing. It was really starting to put me off. Nobody in Roca looked at me like that.

"Don't have too much. I don't want you passing out in bed later."

He didn't blush this time, or at least I couldn't tell if he did beyond the flush that already sat in his cheeks, but he did grin.

"You are very forward," he mused, letting his baritone resonate.

He put his mug down on the table, and I noticed fingerprints melted into the frost on the glass. I picked up the mug to examine the peculiar sight, then slapped it to my temple and felt the sweet relief as the chill numbed a little.

"You seem to be a skilled shaman."

He nodded slowly. His eyes were focused on me, but his mind seemed to be wandering.

"Why visit Ukaleq if you still have your god's power?"

"I do not. I am godless now, much like the Unkubernan, but that's a private matter." He frowned, then gestured to my head. "May I?"

I pulled the mug from my temple and cocked my head, not sure what he meant. He reached forward and placed his hand on the top of my head. After a moment, I realized the ache was gone, and it was no longer a strain to keep my eyes open.

"Better?" he asked.

"What else did you do?" I studied his face for any signs of treachery.

"Shaman healing trick." He smiled. "I asked your body what was wrong and convinced it to prioritize fixing it."

"How do you do these things without a god's authority?" I asked.

"I didn't do anything. I just gave your body some advice."

"A little invasive, don't you think?"

He laughed. "Have you never been healed by a shaman before?"

"No. Most shamans who pilgrimage to the goddess Ukaleq are powerless."

"Hmm," he mused. "If you get so many pilgrims, then I'm surprised your musician is not familiar with the ballad of Paho."

"Monte can play anything," I said with a wink to the musician. "But we're far enough out that even the same songs will have different names. Describe it."

Monte did not break his tune as he leaned over from the stage to listen for Denali's description.

"Ah, how to describe the ballad of Paho. Let me think." Denali took a big drink and let out a sigh. "It is a hopeful tune, even if you do not have the words. It is fast and builds even more so. It has notes that slide into one another. I have never seen it played on strings like yours or by one person."

Monte began plucking a tune. Denali cocked his head, listening intently. As Monte began to strum, Denali smiled again.

"Yes! Well done."

I had never heard Monte play this one, and it really did get faster and faster. Monte's fingers looked like a blur at both ends, but the man appeared completely at ease, as though he had been playing the same song in the same style every night for the last month.

"Reminds me of home," Denali said to me.

"And where is home?" I prodded.

"The city of our god, Pahokute."

"Your god," I corrected him. "I've never heard of that great spirit. You're a long way from home."

He nodded in agreement. "I suppose he isn't my god anymore either. Are you from here?"

I leaned my chair back on two legs and inspected him. He cocked an eyebrow at me.

"You'll share a bed, but you won't share a little about yourself?"

I kept my appraising gaze on him in case my previous judgment of his character was premature. He must have felt the pressure, as he glanced to his right as though catching the glimpse of a new thought for the first time.

"Is that not what you were implying before?" He put his hand to his chin briefly before continuing. "I didn't mean to offend. I . . ." He trailed off at the sight of my grin.

"You understood me correctly," I finally said.

It was now his turn to level an appraising gaze at me, but his came with a question he bit back in his cheek.

"What's with the consternation?" I asked.

His deep voice hummed as he worked the words to his lips. "I guess what I would like to know is if I received a special invitation and why."

I began rocking on the back two legs of the chair. "I don't sleep with every pilgrim who rolls through town. I have standards."

"And I am honored. I did not mean any offense, but again, I'm curious as to why I received the offer so suddenly."

"Is it not enough that I find you attractive?" I asked.

"With this face?" He laughed as he pointed with a thick crooked finger. "I don't think that would be enough for someone such as yourself."

"You're honest," I admitted offhand.

He leaned forward in his chair. "And you can make this judgment of character so quickly?"

"It's a gift."

His eyes were intense as he looked at me, elbows on the table. It had been a long time since someone had looked at me with such intensity. I hurried to change the topic.

"Back to your original question," I said, relieved to find him sitting back in his chair. "Am I from the Unkubernan? Born and raised. This hole? Been here three years now." I pulled my braid over my shoulder to keep it from dangling off my back as I continued to rock in the chair. "Who is the final member coming to meet you all?"

"I do not know his name." He shrugged. "Yuma informed me he is the strongest and we should not go any deeper into the Unkubernan without him. He claims to have made the trip to Ukaleq before."

I laughed, and he shared a smile with me, but he seemed sincere.

"Tell me," he said. "How do gangs operate in this part of the world? The expression took me by surprise earlier. Has my ignorance brought trouble down on you all? I am not familiar with the culture out here."

I laughed again. "No, these slingers seem harmless enough as slingers go." I looked at the four of them huddled over their drinks at the counter discussing something. "They're probably just trying to make a name for themselves. It's a good thing you didn't come across a real gang."

"I was not expecting to hear so much about gangs and lawlessness. I've heard many stories of the fabled Roche slingers, the lawmen of a godless land, but no one seems willing to talk about them since I started crossing the wasteland."

I let my chair fall back to all fours and leaned forward, elbows on the table. "That's because there aren't any left."

"How is that possible? The Roche slingers all swore on Death himself. How did they break their oaths?"

"What makes you think they aren't all dead?" I asked.

He buried his face in his drink at the question and then looked to Monte. The musician's tune finally reached a crescendo, but instead of a big finale, it kept the breakneck pace. The musician still did not look to be straining himself, but his concentration was focused on his fretting fingers now.

"You seem to know a lot about the Roche slingers," I said.

He shrugged. "A chaotic explained their order to me, and she advised me to seek out her goddess, Ukaleq."

"You met a daughter of Ukaleq? A chaotic?"

He shrugged again and took another drink. "There's a lot more of them out in the world than there are slingers of Roche, and yet here I sit next to one."

My expression was cold. "I'm from Roche, but I never swore the covenant while I was there."

I swore it after I left, I told myself so it felt less like a lie.

"Yet you live by the Roche covenant. Very Unkubernan of you." He chuckled.

"What is that supposed to mean?"

"I meant no offense. I've noticed the people out here in the Unkubernan are self-reliant and proud. It does not surprise me that you would want to honor your people by living their covenant."

The song finished with a final flourish. Denali stood and applauded vigorously before returning to his seat.

Dayani, the tavern owner, brought us a loaf of bread and some greens as her husband began the next tune.

"Are we out of meat?" I asked.

The intimidatingly quiet woman gave a curt nod.

"Sorry, I'll go on a hunt when these ones clear out." Dayani gave another nod and walked off with my bag of empty bottles in hand. "Just tell me next time," I called after her.

I saw Monte looking at me with an amused smile before his attention went back to his instrument. I looked back to Denali.

"Sorry, you city folk don't eat meat, do you?"

"Depends on the local god," he said. "I'm not averse to it."

"Then I'm sorry we don't have any," I said as I tossed my braid back over my shoulder, pulled a chunk of bread off the loaf, and began eating.

"So tell me," he began hesitantly. "To be this town's slinger, you had to kill the previous slinger? Is that how it works?"

I shot him a look. "It isn't murder."

"No judgment intended," he said, baring his palms

to me. "I'm just curious. I have a million questions since getting to the Unkubernan, and I never know how to ask without offending."

"My mentor sent me out here to finish my apprenticeship with the great Vertere. I killed the man in self-defense, and I've been protecting the people and defending the title ever since," I said, chewing through a mouthful of greens. "Ask your questions. I'll humor you. You've been honest with me."

I hadn't realized his smile could grow any bigger, but it did, and he leaned forward intently.

"Rapid fire, I love this game." He rubbed his hands together. "How old are you?"

"Twenty-three, I think."

"Where does the water come from?"

"Shamans used their authority to drill wells thousands of years ago."

"After you all were forsaken or before?"

I cocked an eyebrow before taking another mouthful. "People don't take kindly to that term, but it was after the land was . . . abandoned by the great spirits."

"I see. Where do you grow crops?"

"Most are the buds that grow in the ground. The leafy ones we get from caravans coming east."

"When did the last person successfully reach the goddess on a pilgrimage?"

"Before my lifetime." I shrugged.

"Where does the lumber for the buildings come from?"

"There's a river fifty miles east. No trees grow, but logs float down."

"These buildings were not built from waterlogged lumber," he observed.

"These buildings are ancient," I countered.

"Do you have any family?"

"No."

"Will you come work for me?"

I paused and looked up at him, my plate nearly empty. "I can't leave these people."

"You have been protecting them for three years, and they still call you an outsider. I think you have paid your dues." His eyes were soft. "Come with me."

"Either the chief releases me or a more capable slinger comes along and takes my post. Those are the rules."

"I respect you honoring your forebearers' covenants, but the world is changing, even out here in the Unkubernan. Will you be an outsider to these people for the next fifty years?"

"I have it good here, Denali. Winning the affection of the people is up to them at this point. My whole life has been a battle for survival. Now here I sit in a remote town as their slinger with all my needs taken care of. Traveling deeper into the Unkubernan for a myth sounds like going right back into fighting for survival . . . or suicide."

"Hmm. Your base physical needs are being met, but I promise you there is more to life. Even if you do not see that now, you will someday. You will outgrow Roca. With your potential, you will likely even outgrow the Unkubernan."

"Potential? Because I'm a good slinger? I've seen what happens to people who outgrow their corner of the world because they are good at killing. It's just more killing."

"Very wise, but no. I don't mean your capacity to kill. Self-defense is important, mind you, even necessary in this world, but what I am talking about is truth and justice."

I looked up at him. My covenant played through my mind on instinct at those two words. *To uphold justice as truth demands.*

"I think you are unique. Like your name, for instance. Here we are in the godless wasteland of the Unkubernan, and you are the first person I have met to be named after a flower."

I scoffed. "Or a weed, depending on who you ask."

He nodded with an acknowledging smile. "My point, Amarantha, is that you are different. I see patterns in the world, and you stand out. It feels like a crime to let you ignore your potential."

"Patterns? You sound like that old invoker. You're a man of the world. The Children of Ukaleq that you claim to have met, do you know why they're called chaotics?" I asked, and he nodded. "They command the power of a god with no checks or balances. They stick their noses into the business of other gods."

"Or maybe their chaos is the check the other gods need. Their chaos is the balance."

I shook my head. "I'm no philosopher, and I don't want another headache, Denali.

"I can pay you enough to travel the entire world thrice over, all while staying at the finest places and dining on the most succulent cuisine."

I stared back at him with an empty expression.

"You are bored here. You have more potential than you can understand. I believe we can make the pilgrimage together."

I smiled as I let out a mix between a sigh and a laugh. My shoulders dropped, allowing my braid to fall forward.

"The pilgrimage is suicide. If I go with you, then I die too. Come back to my place tonight instead," I offered.

"I'm afraid I must decline. Perhaps on my return journey when we can spend more time getting to know each other."

"You won't be returning." I felt the exasperation leak into my wry smile. "That's how this works. I get a tussle with no strings attached, and you say yes because you'll be dead in a week."

"I'm too old for you."

I inspected his face. There were deep creases in his skin, and the dirt from travel was caked in, exaggerating them even more. He had gray flowing from his temples, but he was still quite distinguished. "Forties? I've had older."

"Between you and me, I'm 240," he said discreetly.

"Ah, so you're chasing what you lost. I've met a few of you." I leaned in gently. "If you change your mind, let me know." I pushed my plate away and stood to leave.

"I'll see you tomorrow then," he said.

I could feel him watching me walk away. He was likely contemplating what he'd just passed on.

I might still find him knocking on my door tonight.

DUAL

I left the tavern for Winona's laundromat. My clothes would not be ready for hours, as it was only just past midday, but a shower was definitely in order.

There were a few children that should have been in school kicking up dust on the dirt road, but they gave me a wide berth. I only made it a few paces from the tavern before the sound of boots came charging out across the porch of the tavern behind me. I spun in time to see Yuma spill out into the road. He fired an orb from his belt without any warning.

I deflected the shot with an orb of my own. My ears were rewarded with a crisp shatter as Yuma's orb exploded into a thousand bits. I called my orb back and caught it in my hand. My eyes were fixed on his throat, taking in his body language for any hint of another cheap shot. Tokala and the two bearded men filed in behind him.

"That's it? No counterattack? What about all your threats?"

"If you'd been aiming at me or anyone else, you'd be dead already. I'll give you a chance to explain yourself. What are you after?"

"I don't appreciate your disrespect." He put his thumbs in his belt, hands hovering over his orbs, as he strutted out into the middle of the street. "I think I should own this town."

We stood only a few paces apart, but our voices probably carried down most of the street from where we stood. The tavern was to my right, and the jailhouse was to my left. Vertere's boulder of a totem sat undisturbed to the left as well.

"I don't own anything," I said.

"You think you're some noble protector?" He gestured toward Vertere's boulder. "I think it's time someone called your bluff."

I relaxed and looked past Yuma to Tokala behind him. "You should get your babe in line. Give him a good spanking."

"Don't talk to her! Do you know who I am?" Yuma screamed.

"I don't care *who* you think you are. *What* you are is a fool. Look around. You are in my town, which means you are in my trap. Fight dirty and you're all dead. I don't care if there are thirty of you."

Yuma turned to Tokala, and she gave him a nod. He scowled with a pout like a spoiled child.

"I don't know if you're drunk or stupid, but try something offhanded like that again and you will die quicker than you can hit the ground."

He stepped forward, all the pretense of his exaggerated drunkenness gone as he readied his hand.

"If you want a duel, then I accept. Let's get the chief out here."

"I'm here," he called out. "So is the whole town."

I didn't take my eyes off the threat, but I knew the commotion had likely drawn Denali's attention as well.

"Ask your boss. Either you die or you take over as slinger of this town."

Yuma spat into the dirt and ground it into a muddy paste with his boot. "I don't need his permission."

Tokala grabbed him by the arm, attempting to chide him, but he shrugged her off.

"I'm calling you out, girl. I'm gonna make an example of your disrespect. This backdesert town hasn't caught up with the times yet. The Kingmakers are taking charge of the Unkubernan, and my father will lead. That makes me your prince." He performed a mocking bow to the people watching.

The townspeople began to murmur.

"We don't need a king!" someone shouted.

"The people here won't tolerate it. Kill our slinger and you'll face every shot in this town," the chief called out.

"We follow the noble path," I said to the chief without looking away from Yuma. "I'll stick to the covenant. If he kills me, then you let him walk."

I gave Yuma a nod and stood at an angle to him, my front hand hovering over an orb on my waist. My connection to the orb was coiled so tight I could feel the tension through my whole arm itching to release. My back hand lay across my lower back over three more orbs in case his men tried anything else. *I will only kill when proof of truth warrants,* I recited in my mind. "Your move, boy."

He glared at me and kept fidgeting. I had seen that play before. He was keeping my attention focused on his draw while one of his men took the first shot.

Two different exaggerated movements went off from either side of Yuma—the two bearded men. With my back hand, I launched orbs at both of them. Yuma never so much as saw me twitch. He jumped when both of his men fell to the ground beside him, holes piercing their hearts and blood pooling in the dirt. Their orbs lost momentum right off their hips and clattered to the ground.

Tokala backed toward Denali on the tavern porch. Tears ran down her face, making the long scar shimmer as she shook her head repeatedly.

"Please, no, not like this," she whimpered.

"Is this the part where we all respect you more? With cheap shots?" I knew better than to antagonize. "Walk away, Yuma. You know where I'm from. You know a duel of speed is not something you can win against a slinger from Roche. Unless you know the Noble Forms, this isn't even a real duel; it's an execution."

"I don't need your silly dances to win a fight." He shuffled his feet in awkward motions, mocking the traditional Roche stances, and juggled two of his orbs in the air like some sort of jester before slapping them back to his hip. "I'm faster than any slinger from Roche. I've killed plenty. It doesn't matter how you play the game; it only matters who wins!" he screamed in spectacle for the captive audience. "I heard what you did to this town's last slinger. The people here say he was a true slinger of Roche. He wasn't just sworn to the covenant; he could wield a boulder and everything. You've let your cheap victory go to your head!"

I let out a troubled sigh at how quickly the town had managed to gossip about me to a gang that had rolled in only a few hours prior. It had most likely been some of the elders digging for scraps of information about the outside world.

"That's cute." I pointed with my back hand to the scuff marks in the dirt from his dance. My front hand still held the coiled connection for a speed shot. "Did you not hear your orb shatter against mine just a moment ago? You may have fought someone claiming to be from Roche and attempting the Noble Forms for a real duel, but if your orb shatters so easily, then you've never fought someone from Roche. You're outclassed."

"That was a fluke. Orbs shatter. It doesn't mean anything."

"Wrong," I said and released the coil, along with some of my frustration with the town.

My orb did not fly toward Yuma, but the crack in the air made his eyes go wide, and he licked his lips and shuffled backward as the spray of debris fell around him.

Vertere's boulder lay in pieces, something I could only do because the man was dead.

"Reapers take me!" Tokala yelled.

There was a black mass that stood where Vertere's boulder had been, as if summoned by the commotion or Tokala's swear. Nobody else was seeing this black mass. *Could this be a reaper?* I was not going mad; I was being haunted by a reaper ready to ensure my oaths were kept. I felt the weight of the red amulet dangling under my blouse. I'd witnessed a few Roche slingers drop dead for breaking their oaths, but nobody ever spoke of a black mass. If this was a reaper, then why was it haunting me?

"Boulders and hellfire!" Yuma's knees looked a little weak.

"The strength of your totem is directly related to your will and the authority you have over it." My eyes darted between Yuma and the now encroaching black mass. "My jurisdiction is the Unkubernan!" I yelled to the black mass, relieved to see it stop. I looked back to Yuma and continued. "My authority is my covenant. My duty is my people. Whether they want me or not, these are my people, Yuma. To uphold justice as truth demands. To protect those that cannot protect themselves. To maintain peace and security."

Yuma was giggling. The black mass no longer approached, but it was not leaving either. I felt a few tears begin to run down my cheeks, but my voice did not waver. "I will only kill when proof of truth warrants. I will take up the mantle of town protector should it fall to me. I will never abuse my power or ask of any. I am a slinger of Roche."

I meant every word, just like I had the day I swore on Death's stone after my order fell. My mentor's words echoed in my mind. I'd received the same lecture every time I recited the oath in training. *A noble path is rarely the easy or popular path. It is a path of sacrifice and quite often a path of solitude.* To me this meant I did not need the love of the people, I did not need greener pastures or willful gods, and I did not need more out of life. This oath made sense to me, the noble path made sense to me, and I could walk that path alone.

The black mass was gone. Yuma began fighting back his laughter. His breathing was becoming erratic.

"You are so wrong," he forced out through what was beginning to sound like hysterics.

He had an evil grin on his face. My experience screamed at me that he was about to do something desperate, something stupid. *Proof of truth,* I recited to myself. Without proof that Yuma was going to do anything, that reaper would swoop back in and cut me down.

Yuma put his hand behind his back, but he still faced me head-on. Unlike my back hand, his was completely obscured. He was going to shoot for innocents. I was sure of it, but I had no proof. *I could wound him,* I realized.

Before I could completely analyze the situation, more orbs than I could register flew from behind him in various directions, one straight toward me. I could not dodge or it would ruin my concentration, but I did manage to jerk backward. All my concentration went to flinging my own intercepting orbs toward the victims behind Yuma. Getting my orbs there first was key, and second was targeting his orbs. It all happened in a fraction of a moment. My training told me my vision meant nothing at this speed;

it all depended on feeling. This was not slinging. My connection to each orb hummed. I could feel them speaking to me as I spoke to them. They knew where they needed to be, and they knew what was coming. They attacked in unison. I had sent all six orbs, and four managed to shatter Yuma's orbs. There was a loud twang from Denali as he deflected one with his staff.

There was no time to celebrate. Heat rushed into my shoulder as blood began to run. It was nothing fatal, but Yuma was moving to rapid fire against me with both hands. I would not be able to get a shot on him in time before he rattled me with his own. I did not fire at him. Instead, I detonated one of my traps. An orb rushed up from the ground at his feet and blew a hole through his jaw and out the top of his skull. He dropped to his knees, and his head fell to his chest, blood spurting down his torso until it turned to a trickle. He was dead.

I took a deep breath and assessed the damage. There'd been no casualties, but Tali was bleeding. Of course the one man whose job it was to patch people up would be the one to get injured.

There was some applause from the townsfolk. A few of the kids cheered in amusement. Tokala rushed toward Yuma's body and looked to Denali for help, but he shook his head. The chief stepped out into the street next to me and directed his bravado toward Tokala.

"When you head back, I want you to tell the world what happened here. We won't tolerate any shenanigans in Roca. The Unkubernan will never accept the rule of a man."

Tokala looked up with wide eyes that streamed tears. Yuma's blood was smeared across her torso, arms, and lap.

"He will rain boulders on this village. There will be nothing left but a crater!"

"And you've seen what our slinger does to boulders. Tell your Kingmakers they aren't welcome in Roca," the chief said to great applause from the town.

"Chief!" I hissed.

"What? I'm giving a speech. We don't want any more gangs showing up."

"One noble deed begets another," I muttered.

My stomach was in a knot. The threats were neutralized, and the black mass had receded again, but Tokala's threats ran through my mind. I knew I could take a hundred slingers or more of Yuma's caliber if I needed to, but someone slinging a boulder? My mentor, Slalal, and three others were the only people I had known to sling boulders. Slalal, Vertere, and that lady were all dead. The only other person was Slalal's brother, but I had not seen Seattle since I was a girl. Slalal had always said Seattle was dead.

I turned around and walked off. The chief's speech apparently ended when I was not standing next to him anymore. I headed back to Winona's place. I needed a shower now more than ever. There was a chance Winona would patch me up since the "invoker" was currently indisposed.

CHAPTER 7

PROPOSITIONS

After my shower, Winona began wrapping my shoulder with fresh linen. My wound was not going to need stitching, but it would leave a scar.

"Did you really mean what you said out there?" the motherly woman asked.

"Which part?"

She stepped round to the front as she wrapped the linen under my arm. "All of that about fighting with honor. I don't know much about the Roche slingers, but the elders sure held you lot in high regard. Well, except you, I suppose, but then you came after that oath-breaking business."

I looked up at Winona. We had never had much of a conversation beyond pleasantries in the few years since I had arrived in Roca.

She smiled apologetically. "Sorry, don't mean to touch on a sore topic. I was just surprised to hear talk like that."

"It's fine." I dismissed her ignorance. "It was how my mentor taught me to fight. Better to die with honor than steal a victory."

"Our last slinger used to talk like that," Winona mused.

"That's surprising." I laughed.

"He hadn't said it in years. I think all the killing got to him, you know?"

I didn't respond. Denali entered the semilit room, letting in a beam of light and a burst of hot air.

"Shut the door behind yourself," Winona barked with the immediate efficiency only a mother with young boys could produce.

"Apologies." He was blinking hard to let his eyes adjust. "Amarantha, I came to—oh." He turned away once his eyes adjusted enough to realize I was without a blouse. "I apologize. I didn't realize you were compromised."

"I'm not compromised. I'm sure most the town has seen me blackout drunk, lying half naked in a cool alley."

Winona let out a snort. "Quite the spectacle for the children."

"Ah, different cultures, I suppose," he replied, turning to make unwavering eye contact with me.

"I wouldn't go that far," Winona said in a singsong tune, making me smile.

"Well, I came to check on you. I can assist medically. I just finished stitching the invoker's leg."

"It was just a scratch, but thank you for your concern," I said.

He stepped forward and held my gaze—to no effect on my modesty—but was careful not to glance down.

"That was one of the most amazing things I've ever seen, and I have a background in the miraculous, as you can imagine. It defies what I thought possible with totems."

"You seemed to manage with yours." I gestured to his staff.

"Ah, yes. I was quite surprised his scatter shot came in my direction as well." He fidgeted the staff in his hand for a moment before continuing. "I'm terribly sorry for the trouble I brought down on you all. It seems trouble has been following me wherever I go. I had hoped the Unkubernan might be different."

Winona finished applying the linen with a clip and gestured for me to put on a fresh shirt. She began brushing my hair out to start the braid. She looked from me to Denali as neither of us said anything and saw her opportunity to talk.

"Well goodness, it's part of the territory, isn't it? We get a number of caravans every few weeks. Occasionally we're fortunate to get double the patronage with turnarounds too. But each caravan usually has a slinger looking to make a name for themselves or take on the role of town protector. Poor Amarantha here gets to deal with the threat each time. They aren't usually as nasty as the fellows you brought with you, but we're lucky to have someone looking out for us."

I looked over my shoulder as she worked the lower half of my braid and saw her smile.

"Never mind those bitter elders," she said. "Our children are safer with a slinger like you around."

I returned the warm smile. I truly appreciated the sentiment, but I could not help but feel a little annoyed at what it had taken to earn her admiration. This town was so backwater that they did not realize how lucky they were to have me. I turned my attention back to Denali to avoid lingering on bitter thoughts.

"Are you ready to turn back, or will you stay a while?" I asked.

His attention snapped back, his eyes passing over my whole figure to meet my gaze this time.

"No. In fact, I also came to see if you would reconsider my offer. I am without my guides," he said with a small bow.

"That woman with the scar not enough for you?"

"Tokala? She left. She said she had to report back to their leader. She was quite distraught, actually. My guess is they will be coming for revenge. All that talk of boulders, I must confess I'm a little concerned for your safety."

"The secret to slinging boulders died with the grand master and Vertere, but I'll be here. I can't abandon my post."

Winona finished the braid and laid it over my shoulder for me to inspect as she gave me a pat on my good shoulder. A knowing smirk began to spread across her cheek. "So you do believe what you said. I'll finish the rest of your clothes, dear. Don't put them all off next time."

Denali moved his staff in small circles as he thought. "They will be coming for you, not the town. Walk me to my supposed grave, and I will reward you well enough to buy the town."

I shook my head. "Money won't change the world, Denali. I like my comforts, but I'm not interested in putting my neck out."

"Says the woman dueling challengers every week." He grinned.

"Those challengers aren't threats, and neither were the fools you brought with you today. I've lived by the Slinger's Oath since I was a child. It's gotten me this far."

Winona chimed in this time. "Do you still follow that oath for our sake, or is it in spite of the elders?"

I let out a deep sigh and carefully thought through how to explain without revealing my very real bonds. "I was adopted as a small child into the Roche order. I guess I was raised to keep my promises." It felt true enough. "Like I said before, honor is the only currency I deal in."

"But you'll get drunk and pass out in a ditch half naked?" Denali asked.

I shot him a cold look and set my jaw. "Honor as a slinger."

He broke eye contact and looked down only to notice my blouse clinging to my damp skin and looked right back up. I kept the same cold expression. He cleared his throat and looked to the side.

"I will be leaving in the morning. Will you see me off?"

I felt the blood leave my cheeks, and my eyes went wide.

"I'm beginning to think you might be deaf. I've seen slingers attempt it and never return. I've seen shamans endowed with their own god's power attempt it and never return. So why? Why are you still set on going?"

"I appreciate your concern, but I am quite resolute."

"I'll see you off," I agreed. "But at least take a shower. You should smell nice when you shit yourself and die."

He nodded and walked quietly to the back of the building at Winona's gesture to the public showers. I stood and made for the door.

CHAPTER 8

FAREWELL

It was hard to sleep that night. I blamed the heat as I sweated through the linen Winona had wrapped around my shoulder. Sleeping naked was the only way to keep cool. The truth of my restlessness probably had more to do with my mind refusing to slow down. My mentor had always told me to never drink the same day I killed.

Company never came to distract me.

That morning I splashed off the nightly sweat and put on some fresh clothes. I was surprised to find Winona had put in the extra effort to starch my shirts, something she had never done before.

I was met with a few warm welcomes as I came down the stairs in Chieftain Hall. I wasn't sure how to respond at first. By the third smile in a row, I stopped Kamil and asked her, "Why is everyone happy?"

"We are happy to have a slinger," she said with a smile and continued into the main hall.

"I've been here for three years," I called after her, but she kept walking. "That's what it takes to impress you people?" I muttered in her direction.

I found Denali right out front of the hall, prepping his wagon for the trip. My nose burned with that familiar scent of dirt as I stepped out onto the porch and pushed the door shut to ensure a tight seal.

"Are you sure I cannot convince you to come?" he asked.

I shook my head and pursed my lips. "The more you ask the more I think you want me dead."

"I will most likely die first. Take your fortune for keeping an old man company on the road."

I caught myself holding my breath as I soaked in his sincerity. I let it all out slowly and took in his clean-shaven face.

"Despite my occupation, I don't enjoy watching people die," I finally said.

"You are quite certain of my fate."

I nodded. "And the mess you left us with," I added with a wry smile.

"Tokala? I think you scared her straight."

"Gangs are unpredictable. I can't leave these people if the danger hasn't passed."

"Honor bound. I can understand that." His eyes were distant even as he looked at me. There were hundreds of years' worth of alluring stories and adventures hidden behind those eyes.

"Stay a few weeks," I found myself suggesting. His eyes focused back on me. "It will give you time to try and convince me. Time to make sure the danger has passed. Time to share stories."

"Time is one thing I have very little of. I'm sorry."

I leaned to one hip and crossed my arms as I looked for more words that might lend to the situation.

"I have to be going," he said. "But before I do . . ." He pulled a rolled parchment as long as my forearm from the wagon. "I wanted you to have this. Go ahead."

I took the parchment and slowly unfurled it. It was a beautiful sketch of a powerful-looking woman with a long dark braid. She was adorned in a fashion I did not recognize: loose-fitting pants wrapped tight at the shins and ankles and a baggy blouse with no sleeves that still fit well enough to accentuate her features. The definition in the toned muscles was something I did not realize was possible to capture in a sketch. She wore wraps that wove intricately from the wrist into the knuckles, ready for a brawl.

"It's beautiful." My eyes trailed down to the waist, where more wraps held the loose blouse and trousers in place. There were orbs around the belt. "She's a slinger!"

"And yet so much more," Denali said.

I looked up to see a smile and followed his gaze to her face. She wore the symbol of the goddess Ukaleq on her forehead. "A chaotic shaman too?" I looked up at him. He smiled as though there was more to see. I looked back at the sketched face. I hadn't recognize her at first. "It's me," I said with slow realization.

"I told you I saw potential." He pointed to the sketch. "This is what I see in you."

"It's sweet," I said, trailing off into thought.

"But?" he asked.

"Life is survival, and with my history, I have a target on my back for every gang looking to make a name for themselves." I sighed. "And being the slinger here is a little less survival."

"I have shared that sentiment at many times throughout my life. I was a general in Pahokute's army. I've spent my whole life fighting immortal pirates, putting down warlords, and keeping the peace. I understand the desire for comfort, but I can promise you there is more to life than surviving."

The allure to hear more grew within me. I fought back the urge to ask him to stay again. I could feel the sincerity and concern in his tone. "My point, General, is that I've never really thought about a chance at . . ."

"More?" he finished for me.

"Yes," I relented. "Being the slinger in a small town was the 'more' I worked my whole life for. This is everything I wanted."

"Yet you don't seem very happy here," he countered.

I put my head down. "I'm having some growing pains with the people, but they're good Unkubernan stock. I just didn't think I would be so alone when I finally got here is all. I've lost everyone."

"What do you think when you see a pilgrim?" he asked.

"Desperate fools, I suppose. No offense."

"You are part right. Desperation plays a big part in an endeavor such as this, and maybe there are a fair share of fools, but it's really just people looking for more. I was a general, I've seen most of the world, I'm wealthy, and yet here I am. Alone. Risking everything on a pilgrimage people tell me I cannot survive." He leaned against his wagon and took a slow breath through his nose. "I take it you've never met a chaotic, a son or daughter of Ukaleq, or whatever they call themselves?"

"I've met a few shamans, but no chaotics," I said, finding a spot next to him in the shade of the wagon.

"Shamans can do incredibly divine things through their god's authority, but as you know, it comes at a price. Chaotics do not have limits. There is no price. They nearly have the full divine power of a god with no limitations. Now that is true freedom. Ukaleq is the only god who offers that kind of freedom." He stared off into the sky. "I honestly do not know why or how she lends her power without a price. It's a mystery I would love to unravel."

Something my mentor used to say came to mind. "Freedom is an illusion. No matter the power, you'll always be bound by something," I said.

"Very true. Very insightful," he said with a smile.

"Not my words." I winked, but thinking of my mentor always brought pain.

"I've met a few chaotics, even exchanged words on a handful of occasions. Do you know what most of them were before they were chaotics?" he asked.

"It's been a few hundred years, but I imagine they were pilgrims from all around the world, just like you."

"Some," he admitted. "But most? They were slingers. They grew up here, just like you, and decided they wanted more."

I let the information sink in and shivered. “I can count on one hand the number of slingers I would trust that kind of power to.”

“The Unkubernan has changed a lot over the last few hundred years. This is not the culture I was conditioned to expect. It seems most have lost their way, but then I met you.” He smiled and held my gaze. “You are exactly the type of person I was expecting to meet: fearless, compassionate, honorable. You follow a code that conditions you to take on more responsibility, to care for others.”

I pushed myself off the wagon and stood in front of Denali. “I don’t know about all that. I’m just keeping my head low without letting the boredom take me.”

He smiled that knowing smile again, and it grated me with a ferocity I hadn’t expected.

“You don’t know me,” I said more abrasively than I’d meant to. His eyebrows rose a little. “You’ve been here one night, wouldn’t even spend the night with me, and you think you know me.” His knowing smile turned to a slight frown, but my emotions were coming together now. They were making sense in my head and spilling out of my mouth. “I bet you’ve seen a lot in your centuries, but you’ve never seen someone like me. You don’t know what I’ve lived through, and you sure as hell don’t know what I’m capable of, good or bad.”

“I’m sure you have done things you are not proud of—we all have—but are you worried that without the threat of Death you will not be able to live up to your own code?”

My breath caught, and it took me a moment before I could suck in the hot air through my nose.

“How do you—what are you getting at?”

"You said you have a gift, Amarantha. You knew whether I was being honest with you or not. I have gifts too. Like I told you, I see patterns. I do not know what covenants you hold, but I can see the patterns when I touch you. You are different, and when I said I see potential, I wasn't blowing hot air."

"When you touch me. So you were invasive." I kicked at his boot playfully. "That must be why you won't sleep with me. Too much touching? I knew it wasn't me."

He put his hands out to either side, palms exposed in submission. "I apologize, Amarantha. Where I come from, we pursue each other emotionally before we do so physically. And yes. For someone with my gifts, that level of touch can be more spiritual than carnal. Even still, I'm a dead man walking. I just wanted to express what I see in you in the off chance no one ever does." He put his hand forward to shake. "Goodbye, Amarantha. I am so glad I got to meet you."

I took his hand and gave it one solid shake. He kept firm for a moment, then let go and walked to his wagon. As he climbed up and grabbed the reins, he looked to me once more. "One last thing, if you don't mind."

I crossed my arms with a slight nod and waited.

"Why stay at all?" he asked.

"They need me."

"But why not walk away the next time a slinger comes through?"

I shook my head. "You said it yourself: The Unkubernan isn't full of the honorable folk you heard about in stories, not anymore. I wouldn't want most slingers to become chaotics, so why would I trust them with a town?"

"There is a difference between the two, I imagine."

"Well, they're dead or running with their tails between their legs before I get the chance to find out their quality."

"So beside obligation, if the Unkubernan is so bad, why not look for greener pastures?"

Haunting memories threatened to surface with this line of thinking. I swatted them away with a few quick blinks. "Out here, the rule of law is strength and honor. Greener pastures means submitting to a god. I'd rather die." I was not going to undo years of drinking to start dwelling on my past now because of some curious outsider. "This is the last town you'll likely see if you are heading farther east."

"I am well supplied, but without my guides I fear I will get lost."

"They would've abandoned you out there eventually. No one knows the way. Heading east from here is nothing but wasteland."

"Hmm." That deep melodic baritone began to ring in his voice, a positive tune layered over his naturally hoarse tone. "Farewell, Amarantha. Do not waste your life here."

I watched him leave town, pulled by the odd carapace creatures. The heat was already getting too unbearable to stand around watching him go from sight, so I made my way to the tavern instead.

The tavern was empty for the most part. Winona's husband, Dalek, was already passed out on a table. His two boys were hesitantly poking him to try and wake him.

"You boys are not allowed in here," I chided them. They froze and stared at me with rigid postures. "But I'll let you stay if you give me a foot rub."

They looked to each other, then the oldest spoke. "Momma wants Daddy home to fix something."

Then they bolted from the bar. I walked over to "Daddy" and pulled his head off the table by his hair.

"Hey," he said with a groggy but increasingly pained expression.

He opened his eyes and met mine. The anger in his brow softened as he sobered enough to realize who he was talking to. He looked down my blouse unnecessarily as he took in who was disturbing him.

"Apologies, miss."

"You have work to do. Your missus needs you, and I have a broken window at Chieftain Hall." I dropped his head, but he had regained enough composure to keep from plodding back onto the table. "The men will be back with lumber anytime, and the town needs repairs before the next dust storm. Get it together. I don't want to see you back here until after all the repairs are done."

He pushed himself from the table and stood. As he staggered to the door, he muttered under his breath. "Think she is . . . one noble job . . . then bosses us 'round."

I took a seat at the bar as he stumbled out the door.

"Ignore him."

I jumped when Dayani stepped up behind me. "Dayani! I didn't see you there."

"I'm always in my bar. What can I get for you?"

"Some breakfast, please. And water for now. Best to practice what I preach, I suppose."

She gave me a nod and silently moved behind the counter with bare feet. Her massive thighs were exposed through the slits of her knee-length skirt. The muscles looked tempered and vascular. I looked down to my own scrawny legs on the stool.

She came back out with a glass of water.

"Is it strenuous work running around the bar all day?" I asked.

"Not really." She turned to head back into the kitchen.

"Then how—never mind. Is Monte in this morning?"

"He just got back from tracking."

"Oh, that's right." I remembered. "I'll head out to hunt as soon as the men return with the lumber. I doubt we'll have any trouble so soon after yesterday's, but I don't feel right leaving for a day or two if every man with a shot isn't available."

"Much appreciated." She smiled and disappeared into the kitchen before we could talk further.

Monte came from the kitchen right after her. "Did you need something, Amarantha?" He was running a rag through his hands to get layers of dirt off. There were a few cuts and scrapes. It seemed wrong to ask him to play anything now.

"Any luck tracking?" I improvised. "I'll head out when the men return."

"Nothing to the south or east, I'm afraid. Very strange. Almost makes me think the sightings of a demigod might be true. I've got a travel pack ready for you. It's on the handcart out back."

His gaze lifted above me to the door. I turned to see a rowdy group of young men entering the tavern. I turned back to Monte. "Looks like I'll be heading out now then."

"In this heat?" he asked.

I shrugged. "I'll stick to the shade of the plateaus for now." I turned to count heads and only found eight. "Didn't nine of you go out?"

The largest of the young men spoke up. I did not know their names; they had all been middling pubescent when I arrived in town. "No one died. Kilo volunteered to update the chief."

"More like he wanted an excuse to see his girl instead of celebrating." Another young man chimed in.

I turned back to Monte. "Tell Dayani I'll take breakfast to go. Make sure you don't let these boys get too drunk. They need to keep the town safe while I'm gone, and there's still a wagon of lumber to unload." My recommendation was met with a few groans. There were a few rookie slingers among them with a least one or two shots in their belt.

The smallest of them spoke up. He did not have any totems yet, but they'd likely let him go on the perilous trip for the experience and to do chores. "We already got some meat, Ms. Amarantha."

I winced at the honorific.

The largest boy started laughing. "We ain't got enough meat to feed Amara here! You'd have to bring her one of them stomping mastodons to get in her bed, Nole."

The gaggle of boys giggled with a few guffaws. The small boy who had broached the topic sheepishly looked to the floor with red cheeks.

Monte smacked his hand on the counter to silence them and pointed a slender finger toward the group. "Nole's got it figured out. It is a matter of respect. You all had better learn some, or I will have you all referring to Amarantha here as Master Slinger from now on."

The group of eight boys fell awkwardly quiet and spread themselves out from the direction of Monte's finger. A few moved toward a table, and another pair headed to the other end of the bar. The smallest boy stood near the largest, and upon closer inspection they were clearly related—brothers most likely, but possibly cousins. The smallest one shared a glance with the largest, nodded to himself, and then came and sat by me at the bar without making eye contact. I could not help the bemused smirk that grew across my cheek.

The largest huffed and puffed out his chest as he sauntered to the bar. "I've earned a few drinks. I'm the one who killed the beast."

"Only one?" I asked.

His face went pale, and the laughter resumed.

"No, no," I said, hushing them all with a wave. "Um, good job." I knew all too well how fragile young men's egos could be. "What I mean is I'm surprised you only encountered one beast. Not even a pack? You traveled a hundred miles or so deeper into the Unkubernan."

"It was a big one." He squirmed on his stool. "We saw quite a few packs, but they passed us by in a hurry, every single one heading north like they were running from a great storm. You ever seen anything like it?"

"No, I haven't." I looked to Monte, and he shrugged.

"Well, Kilo is updating the chief and the elders right now. You should probably be there too, Master Slinger." The boy's tone was pure business now.

"I learn better if I see it for myself. Um, thank you." I stood from the barstool. "Not too much to drink for them, Monte, but give this one an extra, and give the little one a sample. I like my men with a little hair on their chest." I winked to the small boy, and his face went bright red. The largest boy clapped him on the back.

"One drink." I held up a finger to the rest of the young men.

"No complaints, boys," Monte said, silencing the groans. "Settle in for a ballad instead. I composed something last night in honor of our Master Slinger's triumphs."

"What are you on about, old man?" a young man with his feet on the table called out.

"I'm talking about the gang Amarantha destroyed yesterday." The boy put his feet down from the table and sat up straight. They all stared at me as Monte turned to address me directly. "Care to stay and listen?"

"A ballad about me?" I could feel my cheeks getting hot. "Tell you what, perform it for an audience, and I'll listen when I get back."

"Delightful idea!" He raised both fists above his head enthusiastically.

I turned for the back door to fetch the travel pack and wait for my breakfast. I felt all their eyes on me. I could not be in there a moment longer as Monte started plucking his instrument. The cuts and scrapes on his hands did not seem to faze him. I whipped a few of the orbs I'd left strewn about the alley as traps to my hip. This would increase my munition from the traditional six in preparation for the hunt. I counted my orbs strewn about town as a distraction while waiting for Dayani to bring my breakfast.

CHAPTER 9

REAPERS

Just as I stepped outside the town border, I heard the cranky voice of Tali calling out to me. I put down the cart and stepped out from the rails to turn and see the old man hobbling toward me with a cane. His leg must not have been hurt too bad if he was up and about. He stopped just before the shade of the roof ended, but I stood in the full heat of the sun.

"You're welcome," I said.

"For what? This hole in my leg? Convenient that you could only manage to save the others."

"And that is why you're welcome. I saved you the work of having to patch up anyone else."

"That's not why I'm here." He wagged his cane at me.

I moved my arm to shade my face. "Make it quick."

"I want you gone," he said and tapped his cane twice into the dirt.

"You've made that abundantly clear for the last three years." I felt my eyes roll involuntarily as I said it. "If that's all, I'm going to get back to it. It's hot, and I don't care to be yelled at while standing in the sun."

"You heard that woman. She knows who you are, she knows your past, and you let her live. She is going to bring an army after you. We've heard reports of these Kingmakers. They have massive forces, and her threats of boulders might not be far from the truth. There have been rumors."

"Even if they have an army, they are not going to spend half a year and all the resources to move that large a force this far out into the wasteland. You elders are paranoid. I knew every slinger capable of using a boulder without ripping their arm off. They are all dead."

The old man tapped his cane into the ground three times in rapid succession. "Were there others at your skill level? Other apprentices the grand master had? Your trick yesterday, were there other apprentices who could do it? That wasn't slinging, and neither is what they do with those boulders."

I squinted to focus on Tali's eyes. "What do you know, old man?"

"Were there others that he trained? Did he put you in a family unit?"

"Yes, my adopted brothers and sisters. All dead well before their eighteenth birthdays."

"Good."

"Good? Reapers take me. What is the matter with you, old man?"

My connection to my orbs thrummed. The heat rising in my cheeks outweighed the heat of the sun beating down on me. The old man stumbled backward and fell. His cane clattered off the rocks in the dirt. "What? Why here?"

I turned to where the old man had been pointing and jumped back from the black mass that stood next to me. It did not move toward me. It just stood there in the heat of the day, casting no shadow other than the shadow that encompassed it.

"Why is there a reaper?" the old man screamed at me. "All this time . . . I—"

"Keep it to yourself, Tali." I kept an eye on the black mass while I addressed the old invoker. "The more people who know, the more likely word will get out, and then we'll have trouble for sure."

"No, this isn't right, Amarantha. There shouldn't be a reaper here. What did you do?"

I shrugged. "I swore the oath, just like my mentor, just like Vertere. The moment Vertere's oaths were broken, he tried to kill me. I didn't want to falter like him." I circled slowly around the black mass, stepped into the handcart, and began to push.

Tali began chanting one of his indecipherable hymns. I looked over my shoulder and saw the black mass was gone, probably haunting me from the shadows again. A few other elders showed up and began helping Tali to his feet. He was a crazy old man, but he did seem to know more about Roche and the reapers than he had ever let on before. I headed for the shadow of a tall plateau in the distance, wishing I had one of those wide-brimmed hats Yuma had worn.

CHAPTER 10

REAPERS

My hunt proved almost too successful despite the warning from the young men and Monte's tracking failures. I had a full pack of predators to harvest. The sun was getting low by the time I finished loading the last cut of meat into the barrel.

I looked back to the mess of feathers, blood, and bone. It had been a long time since I had seen creatures like this. The massive predators ran on two legs with nasty claws that could rip you open in one devastating swipe. It was uncanny to watch them move. Their heads would bob on long necks as they ran, and when they came to a stop they would focus a single eye on you. They would talk to one another in clicks and hoarse bleats. Those same heads now lay as bare skulls in a pile. A flock like this had plagued me as a child, and now they were dinner.

I picked out the largest skull and a few talons. Winona's boys would probably have fun with these. I had already foraged the skull for its brain and eyes. Some of the elders appreciated them as delicacies. I was not averse to the taste of oddities at times of desperate survival, but it did not feel right to eat those parts if it was not necessary. They may have been dumb and wild now, but these were the descendants of demigods—not that I was devout. I had never personally interacted with a god or demi-god to know if they deserved any sort of reverence. Some of the elders argued it was better not to waste any bit of the creature out of respect, but I did not have time for that today. The rest of the mess would likely get picked clean by scavengers. There were plenty of critters out here more desperate than I was.

It had been a good hunt, but it was far too time-consuming to clean so many. There was no chance of making it back to town before nightfall, but I could probably camp at my totem for the night. I grabbed the handcart and began to push.

The sun was almost gone by the time I made it to the familiar totem. The massive black stone was smooth and sleek from years of working it. It reflected the moonlight, giving a soft illumination to the surrounding area.

"Hello, old friend." It was certainly my totem at this point, just as the orbs on my belt were. It was infused with my essence, but unlike the orbs at my belt, I had no control over this one. The connection was there, but no matter how hard I tried, I was not strong enough to make it move.

I ran my hand over the surface and walked the circumference. Nothing had changed, but it was dirty. I picked up my rag and some polish and got to work. It would be well into the night before I finished, and as the moon rose higher and the surface grew cleaner, the glow in the area increased. All the while I recounted aloud to the boulder all that had transpired since the last time I had been out to see it.

I told the stone about our recent visitors, about how the townspeople treated me after. As I recounted the events, the surface dulled despite the polish. Totems required total honesty.

"I know. I know. I'm not admitting what really happened. I'll tell you how I feel then."

The dull surface grew to a sheen again. I stayed focused on a single spot where the moon reflected even though it did not need any more polishing.

"I would've made him proud yesterday. The fight was nothing special, but I think I scared off that reaper with my conviction. I didn't just fight the way he taught me to; I fought for the reasons he taught me to."

I paused and looked to the sky. It felt harder to look at the stone as I continued, like making eye contact with myself in a mirror as I poured out my soul.

"I miss him, and I don't know what to do with myself. I don't know how to honor him. He didn't finish teaching me. I believe in my oaths with all my heart. I know it's not going to be easy, but I am so lonely."

My tears fell to the boulder. I looked down and watched the tears seep into the surface instead of streaming off the polish like rain on a river stone. I cocked my head as I inspected the surface, rubbing to see if it had been a trick of the eyes. The tears were truly gone. It had taken them. I did not know what it meant or how it worked, but maybe it was the change I needed to get it moving. Perhaps I could sling it.

I jumped down off the black boulder and braced myself. Maybe the secret was finally mine. I began to push. I pushed with all my might, changed positions, and tried pulling, but nothing worked.

I leaned against the boulder and let a few more tears out. "I can't do this alone."

The boulder rolled back slightly, causing me to stumble forward and fall to my knees. "Was that me? I didn't do anything."

My fingers touched something with a ridge of needles in the dirt. I looked down to find a cactus caked into the dried mud. The boulder must have moved in the mud during the last rains and squashed it. It had been months since the last rain, but from what was visible, the cactus looked surprisingly healthy. I cocked my head slowly as I recalled this particular cactus. I began scraping at the dirt around it until I could pull it from the ground.

My jaw fell open slightly as I searched for the name. Ayahuasca was the name of the ritual tea. The cactus I held in my hand had its own name, which escaped me.

My master had let me try it once as a child, a different version of the tea with vines and leaves. I had not tried the cactus version, but he had shown me drawings of it to always keep an eye out for it. The effects could take all night and were not always pleasant for the body, but the experience for the mind and the spirit was otherworldly and enlightening. I caught myself licking my lips despite knowing how horrible the last tea had tasted. I wanted answers, guidance, anything. All those things could be right here in my hand, somehow surviving under this boulder for months. This was a gift, a divine gift. Someone was looking out for me, but I had no idea who.

I sat back in the dirt and realized that, despite divine intervention, I needed to wait. I did not have the equipment to brew tea, and I did not have the luxury of a safe place out here. Losing awareness of my surroundings while sleeping in the wilderness with a wagonful of meat was not wise.

The fact also remained that the town needed me clear-headed and ready to go in case the rest of Yuma's gang showed up in retribution. I walked over to the wagon and dropped the cactus onto the top of a barrel. I needed to put it out of mind until the time was right, but my mind raced with anticipation. My mentor had always said the gods only provided ayahuasca to those they deemed worthy of their guidance. It was a gateway to the spiritual realm. Gods had no physical bodies, so getting access to the realm of the great spirits through the spiritual realm was a chance few slingers ever received. I had no idea what god might be watching a young slinger in the farthest reaches of the Unkubernan, but I planned on taking advantage of the gift.

Needing a distraction, I pulled open the meal sack from Dayani for the first time and smiled. In the bag, mixed in with the bread and a few greens, was a tea kit. I turned to my massive totem. Nearly all of the black surface reflected the color of the moon now.

"It looks like we'll be following divine inspiration tonight."

I grabbed the cactus in my other hand and began hiking away from the wagon of meat. If I lost the load to the creatures of the night, then I would simply hunt again in the morning. Tonight was a night for honesty and spiritual enlightenment—a slinger's prerogative, as my mentor had always said. *Maybe I will finally get that boulder to move.* Tokala's threats were eating at me a little less now.

CHAPTER 11

TOTEMS

I cut off a slice of the cactus and brewed it with the better-tasting herbs Dayani had provided. I did not have the same herbs my mentor had used with the root version of ayahuasca, but I recalled him saying they were not necessary with the cactus. I poured the tea into a clay cup and readied myself for a drink. Hopefully I had not messed this up.

This was a chance to speak with higher powers. It might have been a god, a wise eternal entity, a force of nature, or someone departed. There was no telling what

I might see. Maybe I would understand the providence that had brought me the cactus, or perhaps I would spend the evening conversing with some geometric shape that wanted to enlighten me to think beyond my concept of self. No matter the outcome, I was obliged to take the trip, but I was also a little curious. With no home to return to, I had become comfortable in Roca, but Denali had gotten in my head about the future.

I took one last look around my surroundings. I was a few miles from the wagon of meat. My back was to the wall of a plateau, and my fire had enough dead sticks to burn a few hours. I downed the tea as fast as I could and fought my gag reflex to keep from spitting it all back up. I took a few deep breaths and did my best to clear my mind.

"You do not need it." My mentor's voice rang so clearly, I looked over to see if he sat beside me. Nobody was there.

I know that memory, I realized. I climbed to my feet and stepped around the fire and walked a few paces.

"You do not need it." My mentor's voice echoed in my head again.

I was standing in front of Death's stone in Roche, arguing with my mentor. It was the same argument we'd had on more than one occasion, but as I looked at his tired eyes, I realized which memory this was. It was the last time I'd ever seen him.

"You do not need it," he said.

I was forced to relive the memory.

"Everyone needs it. You aren't a true slinger of Roche if you don't swear on Death's stone. I'm ready, Slalal. I want to pledge the covenant. I know I'm ready." I stomped my foot.

He was not angry, but he would not look at me. Instead, he looked at Death's stone. It was red, jagged, and shot up from the ground at an angle that towered over us by a few heads.

"How many siblings did I assign you?" he asked slowly. He knew the answer.

"Six." I winced.

"And how many from your family unit still live?"

"Just me." I looked down and kicked a stray rock.

"Had they sworn the oaths yet when they died?"

"No," I answered, looking over to see him still staring at Death's stone but looking far past it.

"Does that make them any less slingers of Roche?"

"Of course not! But that's exactly why I want to swear it. I want to do it in their memory, in honor of them," I protested.

He looked at me with those calm, patient, tired eyes. He simply stared for a time. I didn't know what he was thinking, but my mind was racing. I clutched at the small red stone in my pocket. I was going to be twenty soon. If he did not let me swear on Death's stone in Roche, then I would use the one I'd bargained off a shaman in Micco. This was my choice; he could not keep treating me like a child.

"You do not need it, Amarantha." He smiled at me. "You have been following the creed since I brought you in as a child, even when your life was on the line. Your moral compass is truer than those of us who have sworn on the stone. It will bring you nothing but sacrifice and loneliness. No good will come of it."

I stomped my foot to lay the rest of my arguments at his feet, but he silenced me.

"Have you slung a boulder yet?" he asked.

"That's not a requirement." I pouted more than I meant to. "There's only a handful of you who can."

"Have you even managed to make a boulder into a totem yet?" he asked.

I crossed my arms and kept silent.

"Have you been practicing the new training regimen I gave you?"

"Yes. My orbs are probably harder than yours now," I said.

"Good, but that is not the training regimen I am referring to. The one with the coins."

He fished a handful of coins from his pocket and chucked them to the empty square beside us. I slung my six orbs as quickly as I could, but I only heard the clang of two coins ricocheting from my shots. The sound of many coins clattered to the cobble street, punctuated by the delayed clang of the two coins I had managed to hit.

"I'd probably hit more if you let me use my other orbs."

He shook his head obstinately. "A slinger who has mastered the Noble Forms only needs six. More than that and your mind will lose focus."

I recalled my orbs to my hip and crossed my arms.

"You need more training." He shook his head.

"You're the only person who's beaten me in a duel recently." My tone was bordering exasperation. "I don't see what these tricks have to do with me swearing the covenant."

"I want you to travel to Roca," he said. "My friend Vertere is the slinger there. He is a good man. I want you to watch and learn from him for a time."

I tapped my boot. "You want me to go to the last stop in Ukaleq's pilgrimage? That's halfway across the world."

"This is important, Amarantha. Humor me."

"And then you'll let me make my covenant?" I asked.

"Talk to me when you return." He nodded.

It was not the answer I'd been looking for, but I knew well enough when a conversation had ended. I left that night for Roca.

CHAPTER 12

GREAT SPIRITS

When I awoke the next morning, my cheek lay in a muddy puddle of vomit. I was anything but the serene picture of an enlightened slinger with a clear path in front of me. I pulled my face from the suction of grime and pushed myself to my knees. The sun was already rising and warming fast. I rubbed the caked mess from my face as I looked around to gain my bearings.

I scanned the area, looking for any clues as to what had transpired or what had robbed me of the experience. There were small lines in the dirt encompassing me in a pattern I could not recognize from where I sat. One massive line ran the perimeter in a perfect circle. I followed the line and turned around to see my massive totem behind me. The boulder had made the circle that encompassed me, which meant the smaller lines were from my other totems. I grabbed at my waistband only to find six orbs left on my belt. The rest were missing.

I pulled for them, but no answer came. I jumped to my feet and tried again. I stepped outside the pattern, not caring if I disturbed the image, and I pulled again. My stomach lurched, and I leaned forward to vomit, but nothing came.

"Totems don't just vanish!" I screamed to whatever god had supposedly blessed me with the cactus. "But if these vanished . . ."

Possibilities flooded my mind. I needed to check the other totems buried throughout the town back home. My hands began to tremble, and I struggled to swallow as I braced myself for whatever outcome I may find. I reached out to my totems; distance had no effect on my authority over the orbs. I let out a sigh of relief as I touched them and felt the connection. Hundreds of totems were back in town, more than three years of work, but something was wrong. This was different.

My knees gave out, and I fell prone to the hard ground in a small plume of dust. My hip was likely bruised, but I was able to keep from losing consciousness. I checked each orb, one at a time, over and over in my mind. The connection was faint but still there. Every orb in town had been shattered, every last one of them destroyed.

My stomach was a hard knot now, and my breathing felt restricted no matter how much air I tried to suck in.

All I had left was six shots and a boulder that I could not even move.

Years of work had been wasted, which meant my ability to defend Roca was compromised if slingers came in force. My lungs opened, and my breathing grew rapid. I blinked my eyes in a flurry to nearly match the pace of my accelerating heart. "The people," I croaked in a whisper.

None of the possibilities seemed plausible. A more powerful slinger, an errant demigod, maybe an actual god—these were the only things that could break my totems, and none made any sense. Whatever or whoever had shattered my orbs was powerful, which meant the people were in trouble.

I could not feel my legs, but I stood and made them move out of sheer will. My mind was consumed with a single fear of what I might find. I looked over my shoulder and saw the black mass of the reaper following me at pace. My oaths demanded I protect the people, and the reaper trailed behind as the whip. I ran until the sun was nearly at its peak in the sky.

My run had turned to a shuffle from pure exhaustion. I could smell smoldering embers before I even came around the plateau. I collapsed to my knees and sobbed. My tears caked into the dirt on my cheeks but eventually fell to the ground and dried in the hot sun. A part of me knew I could not take the sun for much longer, that I needed water and shade, but that voice was small. I wrapped my arms around myself and clawed to squeeze tighter, as if the pain might cause my chest to actually rend open.

I refused to look up and assess the damage. The chance of a gang raid leaving any survivors was slim. My sobs turned to heaves and eventually slowed to deep breaths. The Roche covenant began to take hold of my mind. I climbed back to my feet against the sweltering sun. I knew what I had to do.

There were a few walls still standing. The only movement my eyes could catch came from the small flames that still burned. There were massive craters where most buildings had once been—craters filled with blood and bits. The same was true at Winona's establishment. There was no telling who had made it out alive or whose remains comprised the puddles of blood and ruin I now passed.

I walked by Chieftain Hall, the largest crater of all. There was nothing left. The only building with any walls left was the tavern at the other end of the town. I found a small crater just out front with someone's smashed remains inside. I recognized the boots that sat just outside the crater as the chief's.

"Oh, gods." I fell to my knees. "Did nobody survive?"

"Don't worry. Seattle let a few leave."

I jumped to my feet upon seeing a man in military garb step out from the few remaining walls of the tavern. He was a shaman of some kind and was followed by a smirking slinger with black hair that fell loose around his waist.

"Wasn't sure you'd be coming back," the slinger said.

"Where is Denali?" the shaman interjected.

"Answer the man. I'm itching to kill you," the slinger said as he skipped over some debris.

I had questions of my own. I squared off against them, turning my right shoulder toward them.

"We don't have time for this!" the slinger growled and waved an exaggerated arm in the air.

It was a distraction. His draw hand remained firm at his hip. He shot an orb toward my leg for a crippling shot.

I deflected with an orb of my own. His totem was weak, and it shattered upon my deflection. I recalled my orb to my hip and wound it up tight.

"Oh, ho. Still got some fight left in you? Tokala told us all about you. I don't think you're so tough now that all your traps are gone. Seattle made sure to smash them to bits."

The long-haired slinger cracked his neck and shook his hair away from his hips. He had large pouches on either side. He had a deep reserve of totems, his specialty. In my experience, anyone who couldn't master the martial forms of slinging had a specialty or a trick to compensate.

I steadied my exposed draw hand and detached two of the six orbs from my belt. The remaining orbs I left for my back hand in case the shaman tried to intervene.

The slinger used both hands and began slinging orbs my way. They were fast, almost too fast, but they were predictable and timed, easy for deflection. He was going for crippling shots, and even though he used both hands and had a large supply, he only fired one at a time. His lack of training was evident.

I settled into the third stance my mentor had taught me, a defensive technique I affectionately called the Whip. My mentor had forced me to maintain this stance for hours as a child. My two orbs whipped back and forth between the slinger's shots as my hand conducted them. Shattered orbs lay between us, nothing coming close to me. His eyes began to narrow, and sweat ran down his cheeks. He took a deep breath resulting in a slight pause between his shots. I took advantage and whipped an orb into his heart.

My attention was homed in on the shaman before the slinger's body even hit the ground. He exposed his palms overhead and got to his knees.

"I'm not with him. I had nothing to do with this. I swear."

I stayed on guard. The powers of a shaman were reduced so far from their god out here in the Unkubernan, but I had never seen a shaman grovel before.

"I am simply looking for Denali. Lord Pahokute wishes for him to return."

"I'm not buying it. Why the gang? Why the destruction?"

"Denali hired the duplicitous gang. I'm simply tracking him down. I swear."

His voice was calm despite his act of desperation. He was plotting something. "Are gods known to have a change of heart?"

I whipped my two defensive orbs in front of him as a distraction as I lowered two different orbs beneath my heels with my back hand and coiled the connection like a serpent. It was a tricky technique but could be useful for quick escapes.

"Our lord is known for his mercy. The judgment against Denali was expedited due to the severity of the situation, but after further examination we have found him innocent. He can come home."

I did not believe a word. "Denali is already good as dead. I want to know who did this to my town."

The shaman's face turned dark. "Good as dead is not good enough. Stupid girl."

The shaman smirked, and the ground opened up beneath me. His face turned to shock as I hovered in the air. The coiled orbs beneath my feet were now pinned to the bottom of the hole beneath me. My connection to them was so strong and so tight that they sustained my weight as I pushed against them. I launched my remaining four orbs toward his limbs with such precision that he lost all mobility and collapsed to the ground.

I was surprised by my own effectiveness at the trick. I had only been able to propel myself briefly in the past for bursts of speed. My anger must have been fueling my desire to reach my mentor's level of ability. With my newfound control, I pushed myself forward. The strain was beginning to set in as I stepped off the connection onto sturdy ground. The shaman's eyes were in a panic, darting in every direction, and I understood why. I had witnessed my mentor employ the same technique to instill fear many times before. The shaman was confused, and that was the greatest fear.

"Healing takes a little longer out here in the Unkubernan, doesn't it?"

He gritted his teeth and growled a guttural sound at me. "I will destroy you. You are wasteland trash. You are nobody."

I slapped him across the face and grabbed him by the hair. "I'm done speaking to the puppet. I wish to speak to the puppeteer."

"No, please. Don't burn me out, Lord Pahokute."

His eyes turned white and emotionless. The expression of pain and fear melted from his face as he fell into a stupor.

I let go of the shaman's hair and stepped backward at the realization of what was happening. The shaman was now a husk of a man with no free will of his own. The stories and rhymes of shamans burning themselves out on their god's authority and turning to soulless had not prepared me for the horror of the transfiguration. The only real physical change was in the eyes, but I still fought back my gag reflex. My goal was to speak to Pahokute. I hadn't realized he would burn out one of his own shamans and turn him into a soulless.

A guttural voice rang through the shaman's open jaw. "Why have you summoned me, child? You interfere in the work of gods."

I looked around at the remains of the town still burning and drenched in blood. I took a deep breath and regained my composure, then turned my scowl back to the shell Pahokute now occupied. "Is this your handiwork too then?" I demanded.

"This carnage is the work of men. I only seek Denali. He must face punishment for his crimes against me. Justice will be mine." The voice was devoid of any emotion, but gods were rarely known to lie despite the other atrocities they were seemingly willing to commit.

The shaman's body, now fully healed, stood to its full height. I did not let it intimidate me.

"You have no authority out here in the Unkubernan." I pointed a finger at the blank white eyes of the shaman turned soulless. "Especially if you sit by and watch atrocities such as this. You forfeit any goodwill to pursue justice out here."

"Child, I—"

"Child? I don't know what Denali did, but he is in the Unkubernan now. I will say this one last time. You have no jurisdiction."

The soulless moaned before words began to form again. "Law in the Unkubernan died a long time ago. I am a god. Do not interfere with my justice."

"Justice? I am Amarantha, last of the Roche slingers, and this land is my jurisdiction. It is my duty to pursue justice for these people until my last breath. My authority is my covenant."

There was a long pause before Pahokute finally responded. "I see your oath, slinger. I did not realize any of you remained. The gods will soon recognize Seattle as the authority of the Unkubernan in place of your order. I . . ." Pahokute trailed off, and the soulless took a few steps backward. "Do you command this reaper?"

"What?" I turned to see the black mass standing over my shoulder. "Listen, Pahokute. You are complicit in these acts, Great Spirit." I gestured to the destruction all around me. "No king and no god will ever have authority over the Unkubernan. We are free people. I don't want to see you or your minions in the Unkubernan ever again, or justice will be mine to claim. I banish you, Pahokute."

The god opened the shaman's mouth to speak, but my orb hit the soulless shaman between the eyes.

"Proof of truth warrants," I muttered to the reaper behind me, and it faded into shadow. I did not care what else the god had wanted to say.

PENANCE

I stumbled through the desert for many nights. It was more dangerous, but I could not take much more of the heat. I had not eaten in days, and my water was running low. The blisters on my cheeks from the hot sun were not feeling any better. I began to laugh at the thought of justice and the bravado I had shown Pahokute a few days prior, but my hoarse throat cracked painfully at the attempt.

Was it bravado? I'd certainly meant it in the moment, even if I had been parroting my mentor. It was not justice I was pursuing right now, though.

There were two sets of tracks leaving town. One set went east, deeper into the desert after Denali, and another went back toward civilization. The Kingmakers and Seattle heading deeper into the desert was a relief. "Let them die in the wilderness," I muttered.

My oath demanded I make sure the survivors were safe. They were still in my charge, even if I had already failed them. Without knowing who or how many had survived, it was hard to imagine how I could face them. The wagon tracks hid the number of survivors. There had been so much blood.

I tripped over a rock and fell. My shoulder took most of the impact, but it still knocked the wind out of me. I rolled to my back and lay there in the dirt trying to get air back into my lungs. The sky was beautiful tonight. It did not feel like it should be after so much destruction, but everything kept moving. A whole town had been wiped off the map, and no one knew. The creatures of the Unkubernan kept on scurrying, the predators kept on lurking, the stars kept moving across the sky, and a hot breeze continued to carry dirt across the wasteland. My only companion was the reaper at my heels urging me onward.

Air slowly returned to my lungs, but I did not get up. I was not being smart about any of this. "This is your doing, Reaper. How am I to fulfill my covenant if I am half dead when I find them? Why does it feel like you are waiting for me to falter? Am I a meal to you?"

I tried to get up, but darkness filled my vision, and I laid my head back down gently as I lost consciousness.

"I think you would taste unripe."

I rolled away and managed to climb to my hands and knees. The black mass had been inches from my head. Had it whispered in my ear, or had it been a dream?

I heard rustling not far off. Had something been tracking me? I had killed a small flock of sky creatures at the onset of the night. Their meat was gone before I could get to them myself. I suddenly realized it had been more than half the night since I had doubled backed to check my tail. I tried to ready one of the six orbs coiled on my belt, but nothing happened. I was getting delirious, and the sounds were getting closer.

"Amarantha?" The voice sounded so sweet as the figure scooped me up into stout arms.

"Dayani?" I tried to ask, but only a whisper came through.

"Hush, dear. We're not far from camp. We'll get you cleaned up. Just hold on."

I had never heard the woman speak so much or so quickly. It was almost alarming except for the relief I felt in her arms. She had survived the slaughter of her town, a slaughter that had happened because I was not there, yet she was saving me. The woman moved so swiftly with her powerful legs that a cool breeze blew across me, providing a relief I was not sure I deserved.

"Monte! It's Amarantha!"

I could hear a crowd of people, but my eyes could not make out how many in the firelight. I heard a clamor as Dayani rushed me into a covered wagon.

"Applause?" I coughed.

"Hush, dear. I will catch you up," Dayani said.

Monte got to work on my burns while Dayani poured me some water.

"Monte has been busy easing everyone's pain. Some wanted to blame you for the misfortune, but Monte helped them understand that it would have happened sooner had you not taken care of the gang when they first rolled into town. No one can blame you for their arrival."

It was nice not being blamed, but the guilt still sat with me.

"There is one small problem," Monte added. He was still busy applying a paste to my burns.

"Tali revealed your secret," Dayani confessed.

"And in revealing the fact that your oaths still stand, the crowd trusts your intentions, but they all expect justice. I'm sorry to place that burden on you."

"The burden was already mine, whether they knew of my oaths or not." My frown was cut short into a wince from my cracked lip. "I knew it would catch up to me, even as far out as Roca."

"You should rest now. We will talk in the morning," Dayani said with a firm hand on my shoulder.

DEMANDS

It was a few days before I was able to move about the wagon. The whole time I spent cooped up I could hear voices and some of the growing contention. Monte and Dayani were doing what they could to help the group, but there were plenty of disagreements.

I pulled myself from the wagon and joined everyone as they sat for dinner. The smell of meat simmered in the air. Some of the men had been able to pick off a few beasts that had made a go at the wagons. There were only two wagons and a beast to pull each one. The rest were all handcarts, but they had circled them about the camp to make a perimeter. The beasts instinctively knew to stay within the circle of carts and graze at the roots in the hard ground.

The group went silent as I approached. I took in the faces of those who had survived. I was filled with relief at the faces I saw. It was a good-sized group, though not a single elder had survived. Monte had explained they all stood up against the foe and had been the first to die. I felt relief seeing Winona's small boys and was even relieved to see her husband. It felt good to know they had a father. Along with the relief came pain. Winona was gone. She was the closest thing I'd had to a friend, just out of pure pleasantries and lack of judgment over the years.

I wiped away a few tears and addressed the small group.

"Hi, everyone. First off, I want to apologize. If I had been there, I may have been able to . . ." I trailed off, thinking about what I could have possibly done against a foe like that.

Winona's husband, Dalek, spoke up. "They had shamans and totems the size of a house. You'd be dead with the rest of them. We won't stand for survivor's guilt right now."

His sudden show of character was surprising to me. He was a quality craftsman, but my interactions with him had mostly been when he was drunken. Then again, that was probably most of the townspeople's direct experience with me besides the spectacle of a duel.

"Fair enough." I nodded in agreement. "You've all been through a lot, and there are decisions that need to be made, so let's talk through what you've all been thinking."

"The slinger with the giant orb told us to go to Micco," one of the young men with a single shot said.

"I won't take my boys to that hellhole," Dalek argued.

"We have to stick together," Monte cautioned.

I raised my hand to quiet them.

"I've been to Micco. Taking this group there would mean a lot more death. If it's a gang-controlled town now then there is one of two options for admittance: slavery or recruitment. If you want to join up with the group that murdered more than half your hometown, feel free."

The young man with a single orb stood up to speak. "If we don't do as he says, he'll hunt us down and kill us. You don't know what it's like to face someone with a totem the size of a house!"

"I've known a few slingers with that kind of power."

The young slinger stomped his foot "Cheap shots won't work on this guy."

I held out my hand again to pause him. "If you want to go that route, no one here will stop you, but you should know the admittance fee. If you want to join up as a slinger with them, you'll have to kill someone in their ranks to do it. Whoever you face will cheat, and you will die. These people, on the other hand." I gestured around. "They need you."

The young man quieted down. His parents did not seem to be in the crowd. They were likely among the elders who had sacrificed themselves.

"Have you all determined the new chief?" I asked.

"They have." Dalek stood. "But I declined."

I jerked my head back slightly at the surprise.

"Dalek was the chief's eldest son," Monte began to explain but was cut off by a stern look from Dalek.

"Determining the next chief is not a matter of lineage and not something to be done on the road. It is a position that is earned and benefits the community." He delivered a firm nod to no one in particular to finalize the sentiment. "We have formed a council of elders instead to get us through these troubling times."

Monte, Dayani, and another woman stood with Dalek. A fifth figure hobbled forward from the shadow beyond the firelight. My eyes narrowed as the fire illuminated Tali's face. He leaned against a crutch for support, still suffering from Yuma's scatter shot. One elder had survived after all. The old invoker kept his head low and never looked in my direction.

I cleared my throat, but still the old invoker never looked up. "Good enough. Has the council decided where we are going? I intend to make sure we get there safely."

"We have," Dalek said. "We're heading to Takan for supplies, then we're going to rebuild."

My hand instinctively moved to my neck as my breath caught in my throat.

Dalek turned to the crowd to continue an explanation he had likely shared plenty of times already. "In times of trauma, it is important that we rally in resilience as a community. Roca is our home, and we intend to rebuild in honor of those we lost."

He stood taller, his chest broad with slow deep breaths. This must've been the man Winona had fallen in love with, not the drunk I had known. He returned his attention back to me.

"We appreciate the offer of protection, Amarantha." Monte and Dayani both looked down. "But we release you as our town's slinger."

My heart sank, and my throat caught again, but this time holding back tears. They didn't want me. My eyes darted to every face that looked to me.

"Amarantha, as a Roche slinger, we ask that you deliver justice for our town and do so swiftly. The greatest threat to our people is the return of that gang."

I nodded slowly in agreement, allowing me time to stifle my emotions before anyone could notice. I waited to see where this was going.

"Young Kilo." He turned to the young man who had been arguing before. "The council would ask you to be the town's new slinger."

The look of shock on the young man's face did not disappoint. I felt a smirk creep across my cheek despite my split lip. I could see what the council was doing to gain his loyalty.

"I-I will," the young man stammered.

"Lead the other young men in protecting us. We expect you to grow into a slinger who can stand on his own."

I let out a deep breath and tapped my finger on my arm. "You all are really forcing my hand. That gang will likely die in the desert. What do you expect me to do? Finish off the rest of them in Micco?"

"No," Dalek answered. "We want justice against the man who committed the crime. I didn't ask the desert to bring us justice. I asked you to bring us justice."

I shook my head as I processed what he was saying. "You want me to walk off a cliff after the murderer?"

"I want his head, Amarantha, and I expect you to deliver it," he said with ferocity. A few tears began to stream down his cheeks.

"Nobody wants this to be a suicide mission, Amarantha," Dayani chimed it.

"But that's exactly what it is," I snapped. "If all you wanted was security and safety, you could've sent me after the rest of the Kingmakers. No, this is punishment. You know my creed, and you're manipulating the definition of justice for me to die in a desert facing a foe I cannot beat."

"It's been decided." Dalek turned his back, and the other woman and Tali followed suit. Dayani and Monte looked at me with a sadness that made it feel even more like betrayal. I walked back to the wagon feeling more alone than I had in a long, long time.

CHAPTER 15

PLANS

I spent another two days in the wagon recovering. Monte and Dayani only ever checked on me briefly and slept outside.

"We'll be breaking camp tonight," Dayani announced as she climbed into the wagon.

"And the hospitality runs dry," I said with a bitterness I had not intended.

"Do you have a plan?" she asked quietly.

"No. All I can do is survive on the land and hope to run into them. I could spend the rest of my life out there . . . or die."

Dayani went back to her usual quiet self as she picked up a pair of trousers and some thread to head back outside.

"Are you two avoiding me?" I asked.

She stopped and turned back to me. "Don't you prefer to be alone? Did you want company?"

She gestured to the wagon bench at my feet. I nodded, and she sat down to begin mending the trousers. She was busy at work but deep in thought on something else. I did not know what to do except begin preparing supplies.

"I've been meaning to ask you," she said, finally speaking up. "This is just me, mind you. Monte has been steering conversation away from this."

I paused from my packing to look at her. She sat for a while before continuing.

"Knowing how totems work, you should have known that night that yours were being destroyed. That we were in trouble. Why didn't you come sooner? Were you just that far away, or . . . ?"

The woman trailed off, looking for other reasons but failing to find any. She was at least trying to give me the benefit of the doubt.

"I found something while I was out there." I hesitated before deciding to explain ayahuasca. "There is a very rare root that can provide divine guidance. I found it and attempted to use it, but I failed."

Dayani tossed the stitching and trousers to the side and leaned forward, clasping my arm.

"Do you have any left?"

"Some." I patted my bag.

The small woman smiled. "Wait here."

I sat in the wagon alone. I pulled the remains of the cactus from my bag and fidgeted with my braid while I waited. Monte and Dayani clambered into the wagon with broad smiles across their faces.

"There it is. It looks like there is enough," Monte said to Dayani.

"It doesn't work. I tried. I sat through some dream-like memories and woke up the next morning covered in vomit."

Monte fidgeted in his seat, nearly bursting to explain. "You did it wrong. You likely prepared it like you would a root, yes? The cactus is purer. The ingredients are all self-contained."

His smile was broad, as if I were supposed to understand something.

"This is your answer," Dayani explained.

Her face beamed with excitement as Monte cut a slice from the cactus. He squeezed the juices out and dropped the pulp into a kettle, then licked his fingers clean.

"With this, you will find them. The root that you are familiar with can be used for spiritual conversation, which was most likely your previous experience in Roche. This cactus can be used for spiritual pursuit. This will allow you to spirit walk to what matters most. You'll find them."

"I don't understand," I said.

"The spiritual realm," Dayani said. "Ayahuasca is a gateway for the untrained. When prepared properly, the root allows for conversations across any distance. The cactus you have here allows you to walk the realm, but when prepared wrong, the side effects can be off-putting, like your own experience."

I marveled for a moment at how quickly Dayani could speak and how much she had to say. They were both so excited at the opportunity to help, their smiles were contagious. I found one creeping in, threatening to reopen my split lip, but I was not actually happy. This was going to find me a more direct path to my certain death. They seemed to sense my hesitation, and their smiles dwindled.

"It could show you his corpse," Monte added. "Then this turns into a fetch quest. Still dangerous, but no battle. Your oaths ask you to uphold justice as truth demands. Roca was your charge, and it was destroyed. The truth cannot be ignored."

I felt my lip begin to pout and sucked it back in. Monte's eyes grew softer as he continued.

"Upholding justice is ambiguous, and I am sorry the council ended up on the definition we did, but I do believe the people need that man's head. They need closure. I would consider that justice."

I nodded in agreement. "You're right. The more information I have, the better. Let's do this."

Monte poured a cup and handed it to me. "We will watch over you. If you see a white hopping critter"—he turned to Dayani, and they nodded to each other—"you can follow its general direction, but only after you've figured out what you are looking for. Do not wait for it; you will be faster."

I lifted the cup, but Dayani caught my wrist. "No, wait." She turned to Monte. "Shouldn't we get Tali?"

"Why would we need him?" I asked.

Monte contemplated for a moment. "Yes, I suppose we should. There have been shamans in the area, and who knows what trouble they may have brought with them."

"Is this dangerous?" I asked.

The couple turned to look to me. Dayani moved her head in a motion teetering between a nod and shake. Monte scrunched his brow.

"Yes and no," he said. "In the same way that sleeping is not dangerous unless there is a venomous creature in your bed."

I looked down at the cup I was about to drink from. "How do I make sure there are no venomous creatures in my bed?"

"With an invoker," Dayani said with an apologetic expression.

"Fine. Get Tali," I said.

I took a few sips of the drink and laid my head down just in time before I drifted off. I wanted to be unconscious before Tali showed up. The brew was much more powerful and immediate than the root-based ayahuasca I had tried with my mentor.

When I opened my eyes, I was staring up into the sky. It was daylight, but I could see the sky as it looked at night. I sat up and looked down to see my body was different.

"Luminous," I said to myself, but it was more than that.

There was a complexity to my form that I could not perceive or understand. My mind wandered, attempting to see deeper into the substance that made me. Every thread led to a larger pattern that had another thread just underneath. Some threads were emotions connected to specific events. Some threads felt like they might crumble if I looked too closely, and some felt like they were harder than my totems. Before I could get lost, I felt something pull at my attention.

The little white creature Monte had described sat in front of me. It was furry, with a twitching nose and short arms. It waited expectedly on its hindquarters.

"I need to find what matters most," I said to the little creature. It jumped toward me in response. "But I suppose I need to tell you what matters most. Well, I need to find the gang that destroyed my town."

The critter cocked its head.

"You don't understand my words."

I crossed my legs and cleared my mind, focusing on my breaths. Any thought that tried to enter my mind I swatted away until there was nothing but a sense of longing. I did not know what for, but I let the emotion stay and sat there with it for a moment. The critter got excited and darted off faster than I had expected it to be able to run. I rose to my feet and began to chase after it.

"I didn't do anything yet!" I yelled after it.

I caught up to it instantly, surprised by my own speed. We moved in a steady direction out in the desert, and then I left the critter behind. I moved at a dizzying speed. There was something on the horizon, another luminous being like me. I came to a stop a few feet from it and studied its movements.

I did not expect someone so evil to look so pure and luminous. I looked closer at the face without looking at the threads and patterns they led to and attempted to make out his features. "Why are you alone?" I asked.

There were a few more luminous creatures nearby. They looked like the creatures that had been pulling Denali's wagon. His likeness suddenly shined through the luminous man before me.

"Denali? Why would I find you? I'm supposed to find what I . . . How is this fool supposed to help me?"

I looked over my shoulder for any sign of the white critter and plopped myself down in the dirt again. I looked back at the luminous figure again and saw Denali's staff. It had a similar luminosity and color as him.

"I barely know him," I said, looking for someone to blame. "He isn't going to help me fulfill my creed. Hello?" I called out.

I found myself studying his luminous form. I could almost hear the melodious tune in his voice the deeper I stared, but there was something wrong too. Parts of him were not shining like the rest. My gaze fell deeper into him, but I was pulled out by a sinking feeling in my gut. Someone was watching me.

I looked over my shoulder and saw another luminous being. Distance was hard to determine, but I could tell he was very far away. I studied the form like I had Denali's, but this one was different. In looking into Denali's form, it had been curiosity that pulled me in deeper. This new form was something else, something grim. I could not look away, like when a beast took down its prey with gruesome ferocity. I found it hard not to watch.

Without even taking a step, I was pulled to the second figure that had been watching me. I found myself on my feet standing near him. Denali was nowhere to be seen. The figure was trailed by a massive boulder that radiated a luminous black. The figure looked similar to me and Denali, but his hands, heart, and eyes dripped the same black as his massive totem. He looked to me and smiled. Blackness oozed from his mouth and dribbled down his chin.

"Thank you," he said to me.

A great luminous serpent flew between us and knocked me backward so hard and so fast that when I blinked, I realized I was lying back where I had started.

I sat up, heart racing, ready to fight.

"She's back!" Monte yelled, holding me by the shoulders.

I realized he was pinning me down as something with bristles smacked my forehead. "I'm fine!" I yelled.

Chanting that had been in my ear came to a stop. Tali scooted himself to the edge of the wagon without a word and dropped below the flaps. Dayani came back into the wagon, opening the flaps wide and revealing the darkness outside.

"Did you find him?" she asked.

I looked around to gain my bearings. I got to my feet and jumped outside the wagon. "They're that direction. I need to go that way," I said to them as they followed me out. The camp was empty; only the four of us remained. "He was terrifying. I-I don't know how to do this."

I sat down in the dirt and hugged my knees to my chest.

"Let's take her somewhere else," Dayani said. "We don't need justice. We can start somewhere new."

"Start somewhere new again?" Monte asked. "She has no choice, Dayani. She is sworn to her oath."

I could see Tali's face light up from his pipe a few paces away. He was leaning against his crutch and likely still in earshot. I climbed to my feet, forcing the weakness from my legs with movement. I set my jaw and clenched my fists. I marched over to my things and tossed a sack over my shoulder.

"Will you two be all right to catch up to the others?"

Monte nodded as he held Dayani under his arm.

"Thank you for everything, not just today, but for the last three years in Roca. I know I haven't been the most pleasant person or the ideal slinger."

Monte shook his head and waved his hand. "There is nothing to thank us for. We all grieve and deal with trauma differently. You wanted to be alone, and we respected that."

"Well, then an apology. I'm sorry I didn't trust you both sooner."

"May you walk the noble path," Monte said with a smile.

Hearing the traditional Roche farewell gave me pause. I turned to walk in the direction of my vision. Whether it was toward Denali or the threat, I was not yet sure.

I could hear Dayani crying softly. The woman had cooked most of my meals over the last few years, but we still hardly knew each other. She must've truly believed I was walking to my death; I certainly did. I called out my farewell without looking back.

"Safe travels, you two."

I walked into the desert alone.

DEMIGODS

It took me more than a week of traveling at night to reach the river the men of Roca traditionally pulled our lumber from. I was stalked a few times by the various beasts that roamed the Unkubernan. A pack of creatures I had never seen before even attempted a go at me, but a few hard thumps from an orb sent them running.

Beyond this river was where most never returned. I took off my boots and refilled my waterskins as I crossed. I rubbed away the thick sweaty grime that had been caking into my thighs and the pits of my arms. Chafing was a real concern when covering large distances, but the clothes

Winona had prepared for me before her murder were well fitted.

Guilt pained me at the thought of Winona while I sat letting my feet dry. I looked back toward where I thought the town had been, but there was nothing to see at this distance. All there was to do was keep moving forward.

I continued on from the river, and the terrain began to slope downward. The dry ground began to show large cracks in the dirt, and rocks began to form in seemingly unnatural ways, as though they had been stacked. As the sun began to rise, the light revealed fissures in the land that stretched off into the horizon. The fissures looked too wide to be crossed. I was overlooking a seemingly endless labyrinth.

As I descended farther, it became apparent that the only way forward was to traverse the winding chasms. There were no bridges to cross the plateaus above. My floating trick with the orbs was not sustainable. The more I did it and the farther the distance, the more likely I would be to break a leg or fall to my death.

When the fissures became too wide to leap across, but before they were too deep to descend carefully, I lowered myself down and waited for nightfall. In the winding passage of the chasms, the stars would be my only guide.

As night fell, I gained my bearings using the stars and began making my way through the chasm. There was an odd arch ahead as I walked. It was not near enough to the surface to be a bridge. It sat nearly halfway between me and the plateau above. It was very curious; like the stacked stones I'd seen before, it too looked unnaturally placed.

As I walked under the arch, I noticed a bend in my path farther ahead. The bend would cause me to go off course from the general direction my vision had revealed to me. I looked up to double-check my bearings with the visible stars, but they were different. Not that my angle had changed or the stars had continued their move through the night sky, but they were completely different stars than what I had been looking directly up to only moments before. I knew these stars. They were farther north in the sky than the stars I had been watching.

I spun on my heel to look at the archway I had just walked through, but I saw nothing except the chasm wall. I ran my fingers along the wall and looked for any sign of where I may have come through.

"Damn." I kicked the red stone wall. "Portals."

Portals were the subject of many campfire stories, but this would be my first experience. If there were one-way portals throughout the chasms, then I could wander for the rest of my life out here with no way back. My pursuit of justice now meant aimlessly wandering for the rest of my life, or at least until I died of thirst. I stood at the dead end of a chasm on the other end of a desert with only one direction to go. I marched forward until the next arch appeared, with no option but to pass through.

I instinctively looked up as I passed through to try and place myself, but I was met with open sky, not a narrow view. I looked around to find there were no chasm walls surrounding me. Instead, I stood at the foot of steep white cliffs, a drastic change of view from the red chasm walls. The ground was littered in white rocks ranging from plentiful pebbles to massive boulders. Behind me stood the red desert plateaus and a few different chasm entrances.

Upon closer inspection, I found a stairway cut into the white cliffs. As I stepped closer, one of the white boulders opened its lids to reveal glowing yellow eyes. I jumped back and readied some orbs.

"Which god do you serve?" I called out.

The massive boulder of a head lifted, revealing a ribbed belly that ran down like a thick rope into a coil. The beast parted its lips and flicked its tongue before speaking.

"Thank you for not shooting. I did not mean to alarm you."

"Your eyes are glowing. Which god influences you?"

"Hmm," it said with an accented hiss. "You've never met a demigod, I presume? My creator gave up on this world a very long time ago. No one controls me."

I dropped out of my stance and stood up straight. "Oh. I'm sorry for your loss?" I was not sure what to make of the statement. The creature did not give any response. "I'm Amarantha," I finally said under its stare.

"Brule," it responded after a moment.

"Is this the way to the goddess Ukaleq?"

"It is," the giant creature responded.

"I see." I looked back over my shoulder to the chasms I'd ccme from and huffed. "Sorry to disturb you, Brule."

"Where are you going, Amarantha?"

I stopped and turned back to face Brule. "I seek justice. If I survive, maybe I'll make it back here."

"You. You're a Roche slinger," the creature said with surprising energy. It slithered away from the staircase and put its white body between me and the red rocks of the chasm walls. "I've not seen a Roche slinger in quite some time."

"I'm the last one."

"And you did not come to release yourself from your bonds?"

I shook my head at the notion. "What are you talking about?"

"This is where Roche slingers come to retire, dear. If you climb those steps, the goddess can release you from your creed."

I cocked my head at the curious information. "What's the catch?"

"No catch. A lifetime of service breeds a lifetime of new opportunity."

"I haven't exactly lived a lifetime yet." I smiled and pointed to my face.

A mischievous smirk drew across the creature's mouth. I stepped closer to the creature, and it lowered its head so we were eye to eye.

"What are you hiding?" I asked.

"I hide nothing. I don't know the rules for entering the goddess's domain, but I know that I am welcome to eat those she refuses or those who provoke me."

"So there's a chance she'll refuse me?"

Brule nodded.

"And you don't know why?"

"I have my guesses." His response was somehow coy despite his massive head and serpentine features.

"Would you care to divulge those guesses?" I asked.

Brule let out a snickering hiss as he shook his head.

"You don't know who is allowed in, but you know she can remove the swear."

"That's what all Roche slingers have told me over the years."

"Do Roche slingers ever get refused?"

Brule nodded his massive head.

"You haven't been very helpful, Brule. Will you allow me back into the chasm?"

He slithered out of my way and coiled back to his spot, watching me.

"You're interesting," he said.

I smiled and waved my hand. "Until next time, Brule."

"You'll go back out there to uphold your creed?" he asked. I paused and turned back as he continued. "Even though you could climb these stairs and be absolved of your creed? The goddess could even grant you the power to deliver justice with surety."

"You've given me options, Brule, and I thank you, but walking up those stairs is not a sure thing. I could be rejected, and then one of us would end up eating the other."

Brule hissed another snicker at my description of possible events.

"You'll risk your life for justice?" he asked.

"No, it's not only justice. There is an innocent out there and even more back home. I'll find the fool wandering the chasms. Then I'll come back, and we'll chat some more. I'll weigh my options when he is safe." I turned to walk away.

"You love him," Brule said plainly.

I stopped and turned slowly to look at him.

"Your vision led you to him," he said.

My shoulders tensed, and I lowered my head to glare at Brule.

"Yes, I was snooping. It's very boring out here," he admitted.

"How did you . . . ?" I shook my head. "I don't know how the spiritual realm works. I don't know any of the rules. What matters most to me is fulfilling my creed, or I die. So if my vision took me to Denali, then it must be for a reason."

"There is always a reason, but it isn't always divine."

"You're saying I led myself astray?"

"Do what you think is right. Save him if you can. There is a part of you that thinks it may be the most valid solution. Maybe your dreams are smarter than you are." He snickered again.

I nodded and walked toward one of the arches.

"Slinger," he called out. "Amarantha, I know your creed. I know what you must do and who you must face. This is the archway you need."

I nodded in thanks and walked toward the archway his massive head had gestured to. I readied my orbs and walked through, prepared to fight, prepared to die.

Instead, I tripped over a sleeping Denali.

CHAPTER 17

REUNION

The end of a long staff hit the ground near my head and shattered the earth beneath it in a deafening crash that erupted sediment all over me. I rolled backward and yelled, “It’s me, you fool!”

“Am-Amarantha?” he sputtered.

His eyes were wide, and his jaw began to slack. Tears filled his eyes, and he stumbled toward me for an embrace. He dropped his totem as he stumbled, and I caught him instead. I cradled him in my arms.

“I never should have asked you to come. It’s a trap. It’s all a trap. I am so sorry. Why did you come?”

His lips were chapped and cracking. They looked far worse than my healing split lip. The stubble on his face was getting long, and his cheeks were gaunt. He was thinner than I'd expected him to be after only a few weeks. His skin was darker and blistering in some areas.

"Drink up," I said as I proffered him my waterskin. "You look terrible."

He drank, then reached for his totem and pulled himself to his feet to dust the dirt off his filthy trousers. Standing there with his totem, he looked surprisingly normal again. The color returned to his cheeks, and they looked less gaunt than before.

"You should not have come for me," he said.

"I didn't. That damn demigod said the portal would allow me to fulfill my oaths. Instead, I tripped over you."

"Demigod? Oaths? Amarantha, why are you out here?"

I let out a deep breath and pushed my back up against the chasm wall. He didn't know anything.

"After you left, the leader of the Kingmakers, Seattle, showed up and destroyed the town. They only let a third of them go. The people found out that my oaths on Death's name to the Roche covenant are still active and played me into getting revenge for them in the name of justice. Seattle is out here looking for you. I don't understand why someone who thinks they are going to be king is so worried about a bounty. Either way, I got your Pahokute to send his shaman home, but I guess the bounty is still active."

Denali sank down to his haunches, holding his staff for support.

"Those poor souls." He stared off for a few moments before continuing. "The demigod, did you catch his name?"

"Brule."

"Brule! I fought him over a century ago on the plains of Alabak. He sent you to me?"

"He was guarding the stairs at the White Cliffs to Ukaleq."

"You found Ukaleq? How long has it been since you crossed the river?"

His eyes were wide now, and the strain in his voice echoed in my mind as he leaned in for the answer.

"Not long ago." I looked up to try to find some stars I might recognize and reached out my thumb and forefinger. "The stars have moved about that much since I crossed the river."

He started to laugh. His voice was hoarser than when I had met him in town, but the melody seemed to be returning to his tone.

"I have been out here for days upon days, and here you stumble across the entrance. She releases bonds, you know. You could have been free of your covenant."

"Maybe, but there was no telling if she would let me in, and you were still wandering out here. My covenant is unique. I—"

He interrupted me with a finger.

"Hold on. You came back into this maze for me?"

I could feel my cheeks getting hot. I folded my arms and squeezed.

"Well, yes. It didn't feel right to leave you to die, and if I don't do the noble thing, a reaper will get me."

He stepped forward until our toes nearly touched.

"Amarantha, if you did not have feelings for me, then 'feeling right' would not be a part of the conversation."

I got to my feet and stood face-to-face with him.

"It's not like I would leave a child out here either."

"But I am no innocent, and I am not incapable, as you can imagine. I will admit the terrain has been harsh on me, but I am still capable. You do not even know why Pahokute wants me dead. I imagine if this Seattle character wants to be king of the Unkubernan, then my bounty is not about money but diplomacy."

My brow furrowed, and my teeth clenched. I could not fight back the visible restraint on my face.

"Do you want my help or not?" I finally said.

"Gladly," he said with a smile and a wince at his cracked lips. He caught the wince and turned it into a charming wink. "I would like nothing more than to spend some quality time with you."

"You're in no condition, we both stink, and we have a very dangerous enemy tracking us."

He laughed again, followed by another wince.

"Amarantha, you are one of the most beautiful women I have ever seen in my two hundred-odd years, but I am not talking about sleeping with you."

"Good." I folded my arms.

"I appreciate more time with you. I want more time with you. I-I missed you. Our patterns when they are together, it's like a familiar smell. I feel comfortable with you. I trust you."

"Trust is a two-way street, and I'm not there yet. You're honest, but . . . What do you mean, patterns? Like in the spiritual realm? Is that what you see?" I prodded for him to continue.

"Yes, actually. I-I love what I see. It gives me hope. It gives me faith—faith in you. I want a chance to see what that future could be . . . loving you."

I narrowed my eyes and searched his face.

"Why?" I demanded.

"Why fall in love?" he said, putting his cheek to his staff.

"No. Why look for a match in these patterns? I saw them; they seem fickle and malleable."

He shrugged. "I do not want to be alone anymore. I have been in love. It can come and go, as you said, but I see something in you that makes me want to try. Right here and now. I want to spend more time with you."

I kept studying him, arms folded, suspicion fueling me, but I found no discernible dishonesty.

"Damn," I said finally.

He perked up, pulling his cheek from his staff.

"What is it?" he asked.

"I believe you."

RESOLUTE

"Will you stop mimicking me?" I snapped.

Denali pulled his ear away from the chasm wall and began fishing for something in his pocket.

"You won't tell me what you are doing, so I do not know how else to learn," he said.

He found what he was looking for and pulled the pipe and some grass from his deep pocket.

"And stop smoking that near me. The smell is nauseating."

He took a few steps back and lit the grass with a snap of his fingers. He still held a smile on his face and inspected the chasm wall closely as if understanding its composition were the most important thing in the world. Our dire situation did not seem to faze him.

"You don't have any magic that could help us figure out which portal to take?" I asked.

"I have nothing but boyish tricks left in my bag. Miraculous feats require divine authority, and I am fresh out of divinity."

I peeled myself from the wall and sat down with the two portals before me. This was by far the biggest decision for us yet. Three nights and countless portals, but this was the first fork we had encountered.

"We need to get some sleep while the sun is out. We'll have shade against this wall until the sun is gone. When the evening comes, we'll have to make our decision on which portal to take," I concluded.

Denali put out his pipe and leaned on his totem as he lowered himself to sit next to me. I looked closely at the staff. It was embellished with carvings and filigree that I did not understand.

"Your totem, you just lug that around? It doesn't seem to do much for you."

Denali spun the totem in his lap and ran his fingers across some of the details.

"A shaman's staff holds power. We do not weaponize it like you all have with your orbs, but it has its uses."

"Then what kind of power does it give you now?"

"The same power it always has. It is my history, where I come from. It is my path. It is made the same way you make your orbs. A totem is a totem."

"Could you sling it?" I asked.

"I could, though not with your efficiency or precision. No, a shaman's totem is more like an anchor. We borrow divine authority to manipulate the world around us. That divine authority is a god's will, and channeling that authority comes at the expense of our own free will. When you do this too often or command too much authority, then you need a way to remember who you are."

I pulled out one of my totems and studied it. The smooth black orb glistened in the light shining down into the chasm.

"What's with all the detail on yours?"

"A result of a shaman's abilities." He smiled. "I could control what appears on it, but I like seeing what forms naturally. It helps me be honest with myself."

I looked between his shiny staff and my small black orb.

"I don't understand," I finally admitted.

Denali picked up a rock near his knee and held it in his clasped hand for a moment before opening his palm for me to see. As I watched, the small rock crumbled to dust and fell like sand from his fingers.

"With the proper authority, a shaman can command things to change, to move, to do all sorts of things."

"I thought you lost your authority," I replied.

"I lost Pahokute's authority. Back in his realm, his authority is nearly boundless. His authority as a god extends to all things in the world, but it is focused in his realm."

"So how did you get that rock to change? And what does it have to do with your totem?"

"Are you interested in becoming a shaman?" He smiled at me.

"I like to know what tools are at my disposal." I leveled a look at him. "This is the most a shaman has ever opened up to me."

"Oh? I thought you spent many nights with shamans on their pilgrimage to the goddess."

I cocked an eyebrow at his jest. "We don't spend much time talking before they march to their death."

"So you're saying we've grown closer than any of those trysters?"

I took a deep breath and threw my head back to let the air out.

"You've certainly managed to annoy me more than anyone else." I got to my feet and brushed the dust off my trousers. "Look, Denali. I appreciate you answering my questions, but I'm not asking out of intellectual curiosity. We're trapped in a labyrinth, and we have a choice ahead of us. I'm trying to understand everything at our disposal so we can make the best choice possible."

Denali leaned back on his hands and spread his legs out in front of him.

"I think we have done all we can for now. We have a few hours to kill."

I shot him a stern look.

"We?" I chided.

"I am not in my element here. I would be dead for sure if you had not found me. I really wish you would show me how you have been using the stars or how you found that water earlier."

"Or how I keep the chasm critters off you while you sleep soundly? I don't have time to teach you. We need to survive and get out. We could walk through that portal and find ourselves looping back, or we could pick the right one and end up escaping this labyrinth."

Denali lay all the way back and stared up at the stars. "Some things cannot be controlled, fixed, or solved."

I folded my arms and set my hip. "I don't quit."

"And I admire that, but that is not what I am suggesting." He sat back up and looked at me. "The most you talk to me is when you argue. It is funny how you have time for that but not to talk about anything else."

I threw my hands in the air. "You want idle chitchat when a threat is on our tail and we could succumb to the elements in a labyrinth."

He smiled that smug knowing smile again and stood. It was beginning to feel condescending.

"I keep trying to tell you, you are stressed about things outside your control. You run in circles instead of sitting down and talking with me."

I stomped over to him and could feel his breath on me as I got in his face.

"I'm not buying what you're selling. You're to cavalier. Only a few days ago you told me you wanted to fall in love. Wake up, old man! We're going to die out here."

The amused expression in his eyes softened as he studied me. He slowly lifted a hand and rested it on my shoulder, and I felt my anger soften even as I fought it.

"Amarantha, I have lived my whole life on a whim. I have fought never-ending wars where any day should have been my last. I am 240 years old, I have no family, and I have used my fortune to experience everything under the sun. I have commanded the power of a god. But despite my self-serving indulgences, or maybe because of them, I have never felt as strongly about anyone as I do about you."

He lifted his other hand to hold me.

"My father always said you will know you have met the right person when you can knowingly look past their faults, when their principles light a fire in your soul. You have to love them. If they feel the same as you, then you have a match made in heaven. I am not talking about patterns or compatibility here. I watched you defend that town, and not just from a gang. You are the first person in two centuries to light a fire in my soul."

I pulled away gently and stepped back. His hands fell back to his sides, but I could feel them reaching out to me still.

"That's my covenant, not me."

"Oh? Explain this covenant to me."

"I swear my life to this noble covenant on the power of Death's stone in Roche. My jurisdiction is the Unkubernan. My authority is my covenant. My duty is my people. To uphold justice as truth demands. To protect those that cannot protect themselves. To maintain peace and security. I will only kill when proof of truth warrants. I will take up the mantle of town protector should it fall to me. I will never abuse my power or ask of any. I am a slinger of Roche."

I let out a deep breath. I'd recited the oath over and over in my head for over a decade, but saying it out loud always made the weight of it multiply. He rubbed at the scruff on his chin.

"You killed the threat honorably despite their duplicity. That was your oath. You sought out the survivors to protect them. That was your oath. You marched into a desert to claim justice. That was your oath." He stepped in close again. "You did not have to give Yuma a chance to walk away. You did not have to give that speech for the town's benefit. You did not have to come out here to save me unless you truly thought of me as innocently incapable. You are a good person, Amarantha, probably too good for your own good."

I cocked my head but quickly stamped out my curiosity before he could continue. "You're changing the topic. This does not help us."

"Hear me out. I know a thing or two about oaths and covenants, as you can imagine. They are open to interpretation. You have put too much pressure on yourself."

"What else am I supposed to do? You're about as helpful as a child out here, and we don't have much time."

"Let me take your burdens. If you believe in your heart of hearts that you need to face that slinger with the boulder, then you will be right. Deviating will bring you death according to your oath. But if you believe there is a better solution, you can take it. With my power restored, I can kill him. It's a sure thing. Just get me to the goddess, and I will deal with him. I only ask that you release yourself of your creed when we get there."

He lowered his head to try and catch my gaze. I glanced back at him, then looked away.

"I don't like it. It feels like cheating."

He shook his head to disagree.

"You were going to let the desert do it," he reminded me.

A crack of thunder interrupted my train of thought. I had not realized it was getting darker. There were clouds forming overhead.

"Oh, I hope we get some rain," he said.

I lunged for my bag. "This is bad. Grab your stuff."

He responded to my urgency with his own and dashed to the other side of the chasm to grab his bag. I felt the rumbling as he got to his bag and put it over his shoulder. I charged back toward him, my hand outstretched.

"We can't get separated!" I screamed over the roar.

He froze as a wall of brown water barreled down the chasm. I tackled him into a tight embrace as the water swept his feet out from underneath him. He immediately clasped on to me. I felt his staff latch on to my back and stick. The water tumbled us around with such force that I lost all my bearing. It was different than even the harshest of rivers. If the water crashed us against any walls, we would be pulverized.

I heard clang after clang followed by a sudden lurch from my back where Denali's staff stuck to me. In between swirls I found a few chances to catch my breath, but we spun at such dizzying speeds I could never tell when my head was above water.

Our tumbling came to a stop as we spilled into an open area. The surf carried us a few feet and then spread in every direction. I pulled my cheek away from Denali's. It burned from grinding against his stubble. His staff rolled off my back, no longer fastened in place. His arms opened and fell to his sides. I looked down at him to see a few nasty gashes and blood pouring into the brown surf. He was not breathing.

"Denali!"

I began to shake him, then listened for a heartbeat. It was weak. I rolled him to his side and smacked his back with force. He coughed up water and took in some air.

I felt myself suck in my own breath at the sight of him doing so. I could feel the tears welling up in my eyes. They mixed with the muddy water I was covered in.

"You brave, stupid man," I said, fighting back even more tears.

His wounds were still bad, and he was not opening his eyes. I looked around to take in my surroundings and look for options. Instead of chasm walls I saw the White Cliffs of Ukaleq's home.

"Thank the goddess," I said as I stood and heaved Denali over my shoulder.

"Don't thank her just yet," a woman's voice said over my shoulder.

I looked back to see a woman with a long scar down her face. "Tokala."

There were a few others with her, including a massive boulder. Atop the boulder sat a man with long straight black hair that obscured his face as he looked down to the boulder he sat on. He wore a black vest and black boots that appeared to be made of large scales. The scales were slightly smaller, but they looked just like Brule's white scales. The man lifted his head slightly and pushed his long hair back to reveal a hook nose. He wore a menacing grin as he sat perched atop his black boulder. It was a grin I knew all too well. He was the town's destroyer, Winona's murderer, my mentor's murderer.

"Seattle," I sneered.

CHAPTER 19

SEATTLE

"I didn't realize you were still alive," I said to the menacing figure.

Tokala turned to look at the man sitting atop the boulder. "She a friend of yours?"

His grin never left his face as he looked me up and down. "You must be Slalal's brat. He would be the one to exaggerate my death. I've just been gathering the next generation of like-minded slingers."

I felt my face get hot even under the chill of the water and the shade of the White Cliffs. I stomped one foot forward but was quickly reminded of the weight I carried with Denali over my shoulder. "You don't get to say his name!"

Denali was getting heavier. There was no chance of making it to the stairs, let alone climbing them. "I need to get him up there. He's dying." All I could do was plead.

Seattle slid down his boulder and walked a few paces closer. "Well, that works out for me. I need him dead, and I could use someone like you."

Tokala reached forward and grabbed Seattle by the shoulder. "She killed little Yuma."

He shrugged her off.

I laid Denali back down gently and readied my orbs as I faced Seattle and his gang.

"You deaf, girl? I only need him dead to get Pahokute in my corner. I'm letting you live."

I shook my head, water dripping off my chin. "I won't let you have him. You'll have to get through me."

"Oh my," he said as he put a hand to his forehead. He ran his fingers through his long black hair and pushed it all back. "Don't tell me Slalal made you take the oaths."

I felt an explosion in front of my face as pieces of an orb scattered to the ground in front of me. It happened so fast I did not see where it had come from, but Seattle turned a death glare to one of his men. "I'm having a conversation."

"Sorry, boss. Habits," said a skinny man with a lisp.

Seattle turned back to me. "I was there when the oaths were broken. I watched Slalal die. How do you still have oaths on Death's stone?"

"You murdered him." I fought back the tears.

"My own brother? No, Slalal killed himself when he

shattered Death's stone. He had a change of heart. He freed everyone else from their bonds by sacrificing himself, and yet here you are. You swore after, didn't you? What a fool."

My throat was dry, and I fought back the contortions in my face. "No, that doesn't make any sense. He taught me the oaths."

"But he didn't let you swear them, did he? And he sent you away right before he destroyed the stone. I'm telling you, kid, even Slalal knew that enslaving slingers to an oath for the sake of justice was wrong."

"Says the man who slaughtered half a town." I breathed heavy as the anger continued to rise up inside of me.

"That's fair." He shrugged. "We all have our reasons, I suppose. If you don't die here, you may grow up to find the world is a little less black-and-white than you think."

He looked over to the staircase and thought for a while.

"Tell you what, I'll let you walk up those steps with Samma here. I promise I won't kill Denali until you get back. Get rid of that oath, and then we'll have a real conversation. You'll be thinking for yourself without that covenant weighing you down. No more of that noble path shit Slalal indoctrinated into all of you runts. You're making this harder on yourself than it needs to be. I'm quite a reasonable man. I'd like a real conversation."

I looked to the small man with a lisp, Samma, who had just tried to sling an orb into my face. He lifted his eyebrows suggestively and smiled. I knew I could not trust them. Denali would not last that long anyhow.

Without warning, Brule's massive jaw came down from above the chasm. Everyone fell to the ground in shock except Seattle, who stood calmly watching me. His massive boulder was in Brule's jaw, holding back the demigod.

"Looks like divine intervention is going to give you a pass for now. Get on up there and free yourself. We'll talk again in a bit."

He turned around and focused his attention on the massive demigod. The other slingers had moved aside and began firing their orbs against the creature to no effect. I hurriedly grabbed Denali and heaved him over my should again. Each step felt like my knees would give way, but I made it to the stairs and began to climb. The screams of slingers echoed through the cavern. Brule's screams were the loudest.

"Die! Die! Die! This time you are mine!"

CHAPTER 20

SANCTUARY

I didn't know how long I climbed the white stairs. My legs went through stages of throbbing and aching until finally I felt nothing. I was practically stumbling up the stairs. When I made it to the summit, I tumbled without the next step where my entranced mind thought it should be.

Denali lay next to me, pale but still breathing. He had not woken through the entire ascent. I rolled off my back and attempted to push myself off the smooth polished stone with no success. I let my chin rest on the cool stone as I surveyed for any sign of anyone. We lay in a garden terrace with the night sky shining down on us, but most of the illumination came from various stones and flowers.

I had to pull my drowsy mind from focusing on the brilliant flowers. "Help," I croaked. "Anyone, please."

Two figures ran into the rotunda. A warmth rushed over me, relieving my fatigue and invigorating me. I pulled myself up as an older man supported me. I looked to Denali and saw his eyes blinking open, then hurriedly looking around until they settled on me.

"You did it," he said, his jaw lingering open as he stared at me.

He got to his feet and waved the shaman away. She pursed her lips and raised an eyebrow as she got to her feet.

"You have done what you can. I thank you," he said to her over his shoulder. He walked over to me and reached out to pull me into a strong embrace. "You are incredible."

I returned the hug slowly, then let myself enjoy it. "You saved me first."

"And I will do it again." He squeezed me even tighter. "I will take care of the Kingmakers and Seattle for you. I promise. I cannot believe we are actually here! We are here, are we not?"

I did not say anything. I felt my throat tighten, or maybe it was dry, but it felt like I was holding back raw emotion in my breath. Justice was my duty, but I was pawning it off for a better chance at success.

"Yes," I managed to say without letting the ball of emotion burst from my throat.

As he let go of the hug, I turned awkwardly to the two who had healed us. They were waiting patiently. Denali reached out his hand to catch his staff as it came hurtling down from the sky.

"Why didn't I think of that?" My eyes rolled back so hard my head followed. "We could have used our totems to know which portal to take."

The shamans shared a look, and the woman spoke up first. "You found the entrance without using your totems? How? It was designed to only allow those with totems through."

"Well, the first time I got lucky." The words began to spill out of me, the urgency returning with every word as my reinvigorated mind began processing events properly again. "The second time, when I went back for Denali, a flash flood washed us to the stairs. Seattle and his gang are right behind us. They were fighting Brule, and I made our escape. We have to fortify. They want Denali dead. Seattle is too strong."

I had been on the verge of yelling. The man raised his hand to quiet me, but he did it with reverence, not intending to be rude.

"Do not worry. Bloodshed is forbidden here."

"I'm aware of the rule," said a grim voice from behind me. "Don't try it." He pointed to me as I readied an orb.

Only Seattle and Tokala had made their way up the staircase to where we were.

"Is that him?" Denali asked.

I replied with a slow nod, not taking my eyes off the monster. "What did you do to Brule? Where are the rest of you?"

"Don't worry, little one. Brule slithered off before we could finish the job. The rest of my men are waiting below. They aren't qualified to be up here." He turned to the couple who had saved us. "I need to apprehend this man on Pahokute's orders."

The old man raised a reverent hand again. "Pahokute has no authority here. You will stand down, Seattle." Seattle bowed slightly before the man continued addressing all of us. "The goddess is away holding council with the other gods of the world. You are all welcome to rest and receive her blessing upon her return."

Seattle turned and motioned Tokala to follow him down a corridor deeper into the palace. I stepped in closer to him and stomped my foot to get the shaman's attention.

"This man has slaughtered an entire town. I demand justice!"

"Was that not your duty, slinger? This is no longer your jurisdiction, just as much as it is not Pahokute's." I felt the weight of the reverent old shaman's tone in my bones. "You can make your case to the goddess when she returns. For now, you will stand down as well. I invite you all to rest."

Everyone, including Tokala, hesitantly looked between me and Seattle to see if we would comply. I found myself seething in his direction.

"Yeah, that's fine," Seattle said with a dismissive wave. "We'll wait for the goddess. I'll take my leave for now."

That was not good enough for me. I shoved Tokala out of my way and grabbed Seattle by the shoulder. It seemed he turned out of surprise, not because I was actually able to wrench him around, but it was enough. I swung my fist up as hard as I could and landed it square under his jaw. His head jerked up a little, but he gave no sign of any pain.

I was not even sure he blinked. He simply smiled, turned, and walked away. Tokala quickly followed behind him. My knuckles were throbbing.

I turned back to Denali and the two shamans. The female shaman's eyebrow was raised toward me this time. The male shaman looked at me, his face demanding explanation.

"Well, he's not bleeding," I said.

Denali chortled, and the male shaman rolled his eyes as he turned to leave.

"Follow me. I'm Yamak, by the way. This is my wife, Rochelle," he said over his shoulder while gesturing to the female shaman.

"Rochelle? I've never heard that name before, but I grew up in Roche. I assume you've heard of it?" I found my mouth racing as quickly as my mind. Whatever their invigorating blessing had been, it seemed to have affected my inhibitions as well.

Rochelle quickly cut in. "Yes, we are quite familiar with Roche and your order. This way please."

Yamak was already out of sight, and Rochelle was gesturing for us to follow from the hall. Denali and I shared a look and quickly followed. We did not have any other belongings except our totems. We followed the shamans as they led us down long halls and through intricate gardens. I had questions, and my relaxed inhibitions let the most pressing fly from my lips, but the shamans were moving so fast I could not get a full question out before they ducked into the next corridor.

"How does Seattle know where to go?" I called out, assuming my voice would carry to them. "Has he been here before?" No response. "Does he have Ukaleq's blessing? Where are you taking us, and what's the hurry?"

We finally arrived at a pair of large doors that opened up to a white stone veranda overlooking a lush green valley.

Denali and I both stood for a moment taking in the view. I quickly realized that the veranda itself was carved into the opposite side of the cliffs we had climbed. Every intricate detail, every column and arch, was a single white sculpture cut from the stone.

The doors squeaked as Rochelle began closing them behind her. Yamak was already gone.

"We'll leave you two for now. We'll fetch you when the goddess has returned and is ready for you. She loves meeting new people."

"Wait," I called out.

The woman paused, waiting for me to continue.

"We lost all our supplies."

"There is fruit hanging from the branches, and the fountains are clean. Facilities are to the left, and your room is to the right."

"Room? Singular?" I asked.

"Yes, I highly recommend it before meeting the goddess. Is there anything else you need? My husband and I have plans this evening."

"Yes, actually. How is our safety guaranteed? It's absurd there is only one rule. What does that even mean? What's to stop Seattle from kidnapping us in our sleep? Or worse? The man is a butcher. Are there guards watching over us?"

Denali watched me with a grin as he leaned his cheek against his totem.

"Don't look at me like that. I'm not fretting. I'm cautious."

I looked back to Rochelle as she began to explain.

"You are surrounded by slingers and shamans imbued with the limitless authority of the goddess. Some of us have been training here for tens of thousands of years. You'll be fine, dear. Get some rest."

Rochelle began closing the doors again but stopped as I spoke up.

"Shamans don't mean much to me, especially if you've all been sitting up here ignoring the world."

Rochelle cocked her eyebrow again. "Patience, Amarantha."

My throat caught at the sound of this stranger using my name. It stopped me from interrupting her further.

"Tonight is not the night for lectures on shaman powers and philosophy of law and justice. Get some rest. We healed your bodies, but your minds need sleep, and you are slightly inebriated as a side effect."

She closed the doors firmly, finalizing the conversation. Denali was already making himself comfortable on a stone bench with cushions. He was lying back, taking a bite of fruit he had plucked off a branch.

"She is not wrong. You may feel invigorated right now, but if you let your head hit the pillow, you will likely fall right asleep. You have hardly slept in days."

He chuckled as I looked around and inspected the room. "Look at you interrupting a daughter of Ukaleq." He took another bite of fruit and continued with a full cheek. "They are the closest thing to gods on Earth. No limits to their authority, thousands of years spent debating philosophy, learning the immutable laws of reality and then bending them."

I stopped inspecting the doors for any locks and looked to Denali. "Well, I bet they still shit in the morning. Except her. She seems like a once-a-week type."

His chuckle was soft, and his eyes were closed. He was already asleep, the juice of the fruit seeping into his blood-soaked and dust-ridden shirt. I rolled my eyes, disposed of the fruit, and fetched a blanket from the room. He had a lot more faith in this place than I did. Maybe it was his experience as a shaman that let him relax, but I was not convinced yet.

CHAPTER 21

RELATIONS

I found myself wandering the empty halls alone. Different fruit hung from almost every branch. It was an endless garden paradise with astounding views. It was wasted. My stomach growled—an all too familiar sensation—and my mouth watered. I plucked a piece of fruit from the tree but hesitated before biting into it. The smell was sweet, and I could feel the juice under the soft skin as I squeezed. I had eaten this type of fruit once before. My mentor had given it to me when he found me. For a young girl orphaned in a wasteland, it had been the taste of hope, of possibility.

"You've been here the whole time," I found myself saying to the fruit.

I looked around at the ornate stone walls and flowering garden. It was probably always in bloom. All this food was here year round, just ready to be picked off the vine. I smashed the fruit to the ground as hard as I could with a satisfying squish.

"Tens of thousands of hungry people in the Unkubernan, and not a single divine-powered person here brought any of us starving children any food." I was breathing hard through my nose and let it all out with a final huff.

As I quieted my breath, I heard the sound of muffled music in the distance. I continued down the halls, and as I approached, I began to hear overlapping voices, but it was not just chatter. It was all coming from behind a set of ornate dark wood doors. There was laughter and giggling and music and song. It sounded like a large number of people. I reached slowly for the door as I listened intently. The sounds of revelry were intoxicating.

"I wouldn't if I were you."

I spun around to see Tokala standing on a balcony across the hall. The sharp scar down her face had a dull shine in the light, making her instantly identifiable.

"What do you want?" I barked.

She turned away from me, back to the view of the lush green valley.

"I'm simply enjoying the views. It's hard to think so much beauty exists in the world. That's the power of the gods, I suppose."

I approached the balcony cautiously.

"We drew the short straws being born in the Unkubernan. That's for sure," she said.

"You're conversational," I quipped, trying my hardest to look relaxed as I leaned against the stone railing.

"I'm free," Tokala said.

The woman looked out over the lush valley with a sea of luminous flowers below us. I felt the heat rise in my face. She turned to look at me, and her face was serene.

"Don't count on it," I said. "I'm gonna make sure you all pay for what you did."

She smirked, but there was a sadness in her eyes. "I don't ever intend on leaving this place. He can't make me. I'm safe here."

My scowl loosened as I processed what she was saying. "Is he going to hide here too?"

"Oh no, he didn't want to come back here in the first place. He hates it here." Tokala pointed to the room the sound of music and merriment still spilled from. "That level of debauchery offends him when the Unkubernan is in the state it is in."

I looked away, recalling my outburst moments ago at the same sentiment.

"He's not above having a good time, mind you. We were a gang, after all, and he's forced himself on me and countless others, but he won't hole up here while there is still work to be done out there."

My eyes lingered on the door. It was probably right up Denali's alley.

"Maybe I was wrong about you. Go enjoy yourself. You seem tense. Just know every man in there will want to bed you." Tokala gestured to the door and turned to enjoy the view of the valley once more.

I shook my head of the revelry. "I have work to do. I'm done hiding. I need to bring you all to justice."

"I'm out of your jurisdiction, I'm afraid, and you're out of mine. It's up to the goddess now." Tokala shrugged.

"I'm out of *your* jurisdiction? Why would you need to bring me to justice? I killed your men out of self-defense."

She looked me dead in the eye. "My son."

I searched her face for anything that might've dispelled what she had just said or hinted at what she was feeling, but her face was stone.

"Yuma was my son," she said as she continued her piercing gaze.

I did not know what to say. I had killed her son right in front of her, but I had been justified. He was going to hurt people; they all were. *Everybody is somebody's child.* Excuses and justifications flooded my mind, but none of the arguments made it to my lips.

"I'm . . . sorry," I finally said.

All she did was nod in reply before looking back out to the valley below. She seemed to be looking for the right words. I stood quietly and waited, allowing her to think.

"Revenge was my maternal instinct, I think, if I ever had one—a knee-jerk reaction. Seattle forced me to carry the boy to term, but I didn't raise him. That boy broke my heart a million times. He was a monster like his father. What kind of a mother does that make me?"

Tokala turned her gaze to the starry sky. She did not shed any tears or even look upset.

"It's like you said. We drew the short straws living in the Unkubernan," I said.

She sighed. "But some of us still choose to walk the noble path no matter the consequences."

I shrugged. "That might just be luck of the draw as well. If my mentor hadn't found me, I wouldn't have these principles. Hell, I was even hiding in Roca after the order fell. I wasn't crusading like a noble slinger of Roche."

"You weren't the only one raised by Slalal. You just innately understood something the rest of us didn't: integrity. The longer you run from a problem, the bigger it becomes. You walk a noble path at face value."

"Slalal raised you?" I said as bewilderment and questions took shape in my mind.

"Good night, Amarantha. I'm going to join the festivities no matter what Seattle thinks of it. Go clean yourself up. Denali's blood is crusting down your back."

"I know," I said with a small shrug that cracked the dried blood. It had bled through to my skin during the ascent.

Tokala walked off into the room full of shamans. Before the doors could close behind her, two separate couples walked out and ventured in separate directions down the hall. To the left I noticed Yamak with a woman scooped up in his arms. My eyes immediately darted to the other couple that went down the opposite hall to see Rochelle laughing with her hand on the bare chest of a man who was clearly not her husband.

My eyes darted back and forth to take in what I was seeing until they were gone from sight. The music, song, and drunken laughter spilled into the hallway, then muffled as the heavy doors finally slammed shut of their own accord.

I rubbed at the dry blood on my arm as I stood alone outside the muffled sound of gods incarnate partying in what felt like an increasingly chaotic world.

CHAPTER 22

DIVINITY

The bath in our chamber was stocked with soaps and fresh linen that had not been there the night before. Someone had tailored fresh clothes for us in the robed fashion I had seen the shamans wearing. Denali had simply laughed when I complained that someone had come into our room while we slept, but it did feel good to be clean, even if the robes took some getting used to.

I finished tying my braid and began to pace. Denali stood on the balcony smoking his pipe while taking in the warmth of the sun.

"Of all the things that survived the flash flood, you managed to keep that smelly old pipe?"

"How lucky is that?" he said with a smirk. "You seem restless, Amarantha."

I pulled my fingers from my mouth and spat out the nail I had been biting. I walked over and joined him on the balcony. I grabbed the pipe from him and took a long drag. The shocked looked on his face turned to a broad smile.

"I thought you hated the smell."

"I do, but I know what you're smoking, and I could use some."

"What is bothering you so much?" he asked.

I had to blink a few times before I could wipe the incredulity from my face.

"Everything, you madman," I said, only half joking as I pushed the pipe back into his chest. "I don't like not knowing the rules. What is the goddess going to say? What if she kicks us out and Seattle gives us chase? Shouldn't we be prepared? We could be on the run in the next hour, and Seattle could be hot on our tail. We have no guarantees right now and no way of knowing what our fates may be. If this is Ukaleq's jurisdiction, then we need to know what kind of case to make against Seattle. How do we guarantee he is brought to justice? Well? Stop smiling! How can you be so relaxed?"

He let out a slow breath of smoke and knocked his pipe clean on the banister. "I really enjoy living. There is a lot this world has to offer and even more mysteries. I could probably spend the next five hundred years exploring and still not be content, but I am not afraid to die either. Even the chaotic shamans of Ukaleq do not live forever.

Probability dictates a fatal accident at some point." He chuckled to himself. "In a world where gods interact with us mere mortals, there is only so much you can control. It is a gamble to play by their rules, but if you do not take the gamble, you are not living. You are just surviving. I want to show you what it means to thrive."

"So you want me to sit still and wait? Leave things to fate?" I asked.

"No, fate is a construct we mortals made to comfort ourselves. I am suggesting you play the long game. Control what you can, but focus on the future. Sometimes watching is the best course of action. The more you know, the more you can influence—not control."

"You sound more like a philosopher than a general."

He laughed. "The two become one and the same eventually."

I turned my back to the valley and leaned against the stone railing. "Is that how you can be so calm? A mixture of bravery and subterfuge?"

Denali let out a soft chuckle and smiled at me. "I love the way you see the world. Yes, I suppose bravado and experience have something to do with it. Bravado has gotten me into trouble my whole life, and experience has only fueled it."

Denali reach out and plucked a fruit from the vine and handed it to me. "Here, I plucked this just for you. Eat. Keeping your strength is something you can control. I have enough rations to last us a few days in small sacks by the door if we need to run." He smirked and pumped his brow twice.

The doors to our chambers opened, and Rochelle walked through. "The goddess is ready for your audience."

"Oh good, I wasn't sure how long parties here lasted. Then again, you only took one man home with you last night," I said as we crossed the balcony to her.

"Was there a party?" Denali asked.

"And they didn't invite us," I said.

Rochelle gave no expression before explaining.

"If you have the fortune to live a few millennia, you may find your tastes change from time to time."

"Well, it's just rude, isn't it?" I said mockingly to Denali. "We're their first guests in a very long time, and they are too busy fornicating to greet us. A party is a party, and we weren't invited."

"It would have been a good chance to mingle," Denali said.

"I'll bear that in mind," Rochelle said. "Follow me."

As we followed Rochelle, she led us past the room where the festivities had been held the night before. The dark solid doors were open wide. The room was littered with pillows, but in the center stood a single desk with a man reading amongst a litter of old tomes. The evidence of the party was still there, but the scene change was drastic.

"So tell me, Denali, how long were you in the service of Pahokute?"

Rochelle did not look back as she spoke to Denali. He shared a puzzled look with me and answered to the back of her head.

"Oh, I've been traveling the world on his orders for two and a quarter centuries now."

"A general then? Or an agent?" she asked.

"I would be happy to fill you all in sometime, assuming the goddess allows us to stay," he quipped.

"That's really up to you two at this point. You meet all the basic criteria. She won't turn you away unless you choose it."

Denali's pace slowed briefly, and a smile crept across his face. As he sped back up, his gait seemed to have a little more bounce than before. I found myself smiling in response to his elation, but I continued smiling when I thought about what it meant. Denali could deliver justice.

"General Denali or Agent Denali?" I asked.

He shrugged and said nothing more as we continued walking the garden terrace of the White Cliffs. As we continued, our angle on the cliffs changed so that I could see another wall of cliff. Hundreds of terraced floors ran down to the base of the cliff. The bottom was obscured in morning fog.

"You could fit millions of people here," I said before turning to Rochelle. "How many of you are there?"

"Maybe a few thousand. Hush now. We are entering the chambers, and a ceremony is already taking place."

The hall was lined with pews on either side of a long smooth cobble pathway that led directly to a statue. The statue was slightly larger than me and very plain. In fact, it barely resembled a human figure and had no distinguishable features, but my eyes were drawn to it. Two people stood on either side, their hands overlapping on the palms of the statue. A voice that sounded like the wind resonated in the room.

"Children, take my blessing and serve each other well."

My eyes refocused from the statue as I realized what was happening. Seattle and Tokala had just received the goddess's blessing.

"Reapers take me! What fool signed off on this?" I yelled.

Rochelle flicked her wrist in my face, and my throat caught. The air was gone before I could either inhale or exhale. It was simply gone.

"Learn some reverence, child."

I instinctively went for an orb instead of clawing for air, but Denali waved his hand in front of my face. I felt the air return as if it had never vanished. He glared at Rochelle without saying a word. She stepped back awkwardly.

"Having fun?"

I jumped as Seattle's grim voice pierced me from behind. My hand went back to my orb, and this time I did not hesitate. I blasted the orb with all my strength, but it did not pierce him. It hung in the air halfway between us. I could feel a sense of calm rush over me, but I ignored the lull. I pushed with everything I had, but the orb would not budge. The rush of calm came in another wave, this time stronger, but it made my resolve even greater to know that someone was preventing me from claiming justice. In a rage, I pulled my orb back. Nothing blocked its path from continuing. Seattle's smile grew wider with every blow I struck against the invisible shield. The sense of calm rushed over me in stronger successive waves until I realized I was on my knees, still slinging my orb forward. Seattle bowed to the statue of the goddess and nodded to Rochelle behind me. As he turned to leave, I looked to Rochelle.

"Why are you protecting him?" I screamed. "You know what he is, what he's done, so why?"

"You slingers are so stubborn." Rochelle sighed.

Seattle was gone, and what rage I had left was dwindling with nothing to point it at. Denali approached as my orbs stopped flying. He stooped down and helped me to my feet. Rochelle left the room so only Denali and I remained with the statue of the goddess.

"What did she do to me?" I asked him.

"That overwhelming feeling of calm? That is not coming from Rochelle. That is the goddess. I feel it too."

"Why is calm so heavy? It feels like pure absence of will."

"Let's go ask," he said as he helped me walk forward.

As we approached, every step felt as though something was being taken from me. The weight grew heavier, but my anger diminished, and my fear escaped me, along with my desire for justice and my sadness at the slaughter in Roca. Even as he held me, both my irritation and my appreciation toward Denali began to fade. I found myself on my knees. Denali left me there and stood steadfastly before the goddess. The admiration I had begun to feel toward the man for his ability to stand tall was sucked away as quickly as it had come. Developing a new emotion and having it sucked away compounded the weight even more until I had to catch myself from falling over.

"I do not know what trial you have chosen to put us through, Your Grace, but we have come seeking an audience," Denali said to the statue, but there was no reply.

Denali's words made me realize that the goddess was doing this to us on purpose. If I could barely kneel upright, then there was no way Seattle and Tokala had been put through the same pressure. This was happening to us for a reason. I pushed against the weight and forced myself back upright on my knees. I lifted one foot and braced myself before trying to push to my feet. In one powerful motion, I found myself standing. The weight was still there in my mind, but it did not push against my body the way it had before. I looked over to Denali and saw his luminous form. His body lay at his feet. I looked down to see my own luminous form once again, just as I had on my journey with the ayahuasca.

"The spiritual realm," I muttered to myself.

My eyes were drawn forward. Before us stood the goddess in her luminous form. Somehow the luminosity was even more pure than our own, and the patterns wove deeper than anything I had seen staring into Denali's form previously. Staring was dangerous, I suddenly remembered, but I did anyway. She was so much more than me or Denali. She felt more complete. Before me stood the luminous form of a woman, but behind her flowed a silky train that looked as though it might expand into eternity.

"Where does it end?" I found myself asking.

Denali's form turned to me and grabbed me by the shoulders, turning me to face him. Then he quickly let go.

"Do not look at them. Look at me," he said.

"Them?" I asked, slightly dazed.

He nodded slowly. "Do not look." His luminous fingers caught my cheek briefly and then pulled my chin back to him. The patterns in his eyes were mesmerizing.

"Why can't I stop looking? I can't close my eyes. Who is here?" I asked.

My mind told me I should've been concerned by that fact, but I felt nothing.

"They are not ready for us yet. Something is wrong."

"Who is they?" I asked.

"The goddess and the reaper," he said as he stared into my eyes. I could not make out any expressions from his luminous form, but his head cocked, and he leaned in a little closer, as though something had appeared on my face that he needed to study. I found myself getting lost in the patterns of his eyes again. The patterns were trying to tell me something, and they were intoxicating.

"Truths," I said.

Denali's attention snapped back.

"Yes, exactly. I am not very experienced in this. Being in the spiritual realm is different than the patterns I see in the physical world we live in. I never found much practical use for the spiritual realm, but yes, the patterns are our truths. I am sorry I got lost in yours just now. That was very invasive, and I should not have, but you are more amazing than I imagined." He looked away briefly. A pattern emerged from him, rising to the surface of his form.

"Shame," I read.

"Good, you are adjusting. Look at my eyes. I will guide you through mine on the surface until we get through this. Are you ready? We cannot go too deep or you may get stuck."

I nodded and read the first pattern that surfaced.

"Curiosity, or is it enthusiasm?" I asked.

"So much more. Keep reading, and you will see the curiosity is insatiable. It turns into enthusiasm, which breeds what?"

"Optimism," I read aloud.

"Exactly. I am constantly anticipating the next best thing," he said.

I found myself laughing, but it was a hollow laugh. The emotion was gone just as it started.

"You're a wide-eyed little boy, but you're bold too. You chase what you want. You need comfort or the enthusiasm becomes frustration. The anger can be so . . . wait. Why are the patterns so jagged here at the anger?"

"That is my nature, but I learned to control it. It is no longer my truth. What else do you see?"

"The need for comfort, it branches. Is this a new pattern?" I asked.

"All patterns connect eventually. You are probably reading it correctly."

"Your sexual appetite is a truth?"

"Truths like this fluctuate over time, but yes, I have a large appetite."

"And this sexual pattern, it flows into arrogance and right back into curiosity if I go this way."

Denali let out a deep humored sigh. The commanding voice of a woman rang out around us.

"Let it be so, Reaper."

I looked to my left to see a dark black nothingness next to the goddess. It had no form, no movement, but still it lunged toward me. It threatened to consume me.

"No!" Denali screamed as the darkness enveloped me.

I awoke on the floor. In my mind I knew my body was aching, but I felt nothing physical. I felt no emotion. The thoughts that began to fill my consciousness were slow to start, like cold coals from the previous days' fire trying to reclaim their heat. I could feel a heat. It was on my face. It was Denali's hand. It was frantic. I could hear his voice now.

"Please. Please. Please," he begged.

I decided to open my eyes.

"Oh, thank the gods."

Denali pulled me in close. I slowly became aware of the tears falling onto my neck. I began to feel his arms around me, his breath on my neck, an ache in my whole body. Physical sensation seemed to return from nothing, and then I felt more. The room seemed darker despite the sunlight shining in. The goddess's statue seemed vacant now. Behind Denali was a figure of light. I craned my neck and saw a woman standing there, but she was not really standing there. My head hurt trying to process what I was seeing. My senses could recognize that nothing was there, but there she stood before me. A mirage somehow? Her presence seemed to be consuming sunlight. My thinking cleared, and with realization came emotion, emotion that did not escape from me. It was mine to keep and do with as I willed. I clutched for where the red crystal hung around my neck, but I found only dust.

My voice quivered as I spoke. "What did the reaper do to me?"

Denali let go and turned to see the goddess. He stayed on his knees and lowered his head before her. "Forgive me, goddess."

She smiled at both of us. I felt the back of my neck prickle, followed by a warmth that started in my stomach and rose until my throat caught to keep it in. Her presence was different from other gods I had interacted with or seen my mentor interact with. She felt truly divine.

"Your nature is not to be forgiven, sweet child. It is I who must ask forgiveness. The will of a great spirit permeates, and I allowed my apathy to calm the confrontation. The reaper arrived at your summoning, Amarantha.

Reapers have strange effects, even on us great spirits. I apologize for continuing to exert my apathy to such effect. It caused you both to lose consciousness, but your fighting spirits kept battling the effects. You handled it well. Neither of you disappoint." She smiled.

I looked to the powerful, experienced, intelligent man whose patterns I had just studied and, to my shock, giggled. I put my hand to my mouth as he turned and gave me a toothy grin. He was feeling her new effects as well.

"Once you receive my blessing, you will develop a tolerance to my will. For now your inhibitions will be askew, but to your question, Amarantha. The reaper is an agent of Death. Due to your covenant, you summoned him with your swear, but when he saw Denali's cursed organs, his nature was to claim Denali."

The goddess gestured to Denali, and I looked to him. Tears filled my eyes. My inhibitions were truly gone now with the effects of the goddess.

"I knew it. You should have told me."

Denali began to cry too. In my mind I knew we were both blubbering idiots not doing any good for ourselves, but I could not stop it. The goddess looked back to me.

"To die by a reaper is to die a permanent death, breaking the reincarnation cycle. I could not allow this fate for Denali. To placate the reaper, I offered him something of yours, Amarantha. I am sorry I could not ask your permission first. I broke your bonds, Amarantha. Your covenant is no more."

I ceased crying immediately and clutched my chest. There was no physical pain, but the anguish felt as though I were buried in sand. I could not breathe. I felt Denali's comforting hand on my back, and the air began to flow again. Along with it came a new flood of tears. After so many years of hiding, shirking my responsibility, and the fear of facing my duty, I should have only been feeling relief, but I did not. Those oaths were mine.

"You were the last true slinger of Roche, Amarantha. The reaper wanted free of his chains to this world. A reaper does not belong here."

"What does that mean if there are no reapers in this world?" Denali asked.

"Reapers are merely agents. Death is a constant force in the universe. You will still die of the curse befallen you if you two cannot meet the condition of my blessing."

"What is the condition?" he asked.

"Union," the goddess said.

Denali's face grew solemn while I continued to cry. There was too much to process. My oaths were gone, and I apparently needed to join Denali in a union to save him.

"I see. Thank you for your time and your interference on my behalf." Denali gave a reverent bow, then turned on his knee, rose, and left the room.

I knelt before the goddess alone. I began to feel shame at blubbering before her, wasting her time.

"Do not sorrow, child. Your attachment to your oaths shows that you never needed the threat of death. You were not shackled to your oaths as others were. You believed in them. Your oaths were in service to you, not the other way around. Take heart in the nobility of your virtue."

As though she had commanded it, my tears stopped. A different kind of warmth erupted from my heart. I burned with pride.

"This feeling in you now, Slalal felt this when he spoke of you," the goddess explained.

The sensation grew exponentially until the joy burst from my face in a broad grin as I stared at the ground. The illusion of the goddess's fingers reached forward. I felt a light breeze push my chin up to meet her gaze.

"Never let this fire extinguish. Go now. I will give you two until after Seattle's examination to decide on union."

"Will he be on trial?" I asked urgently as the goddess began to fade.

"My words are sealed in heaven and earth."

Her words echoed in the room as she faded, and the sunlight filled the room again. I did not understand what she meant, but she hadn't answered my question, and I did not want to break my mind attempting to interpret her words. I rose to my feet and took a deep breath. I counted to ten slowly, flexing muscles sequentially from my toes to my hands overhead until I completed one big stretch. I could feel the scowl crease across my lips and my brow furrow. I let the stretch go with a deep exhale out of my nose. There was nobody left influencing my emotions or my sensations, and I was angry.

I marched out of the room looking for Denali. He was not hard to find. He was leaned up against the wall waiting for me. I pointed my finger into his chest and dug it into his sternum. I was satisfied with the wince and the vocal cry he let out as he straightened against the wall. I left my finger in his sternum and pinned him.

"You've got some nerve! We had a deal!"

"That is what you are worried about?" The exasperation seeped through the pained expression on his face. Both of his hands held mine, but he did not push me away.

He let me grind my finger into his chest as hard as I wanted, so I continued giving him a piece of my mind.

"Oh, it's everything." I pulled my hand back from his grasp and thumped my finger into his chest. "You could have told me we'd lose our inhibitions near her."

Thump.

"You didn't tell me you were dying!"

Thump.

"You said you wanted to fall in love!"

Thump.

"Then you reject a lifesaving union."

Thump.

"You promised you'd get the goddess's blessing and deal with Seattle."

Thump.

"We. Had. A. Deal," I said, punctuating every word with a thump to his chest. I was staring into his chest now. My mind was blank now that I had said my piece. I just stared at the spot in his sternum I had been thumping and pulled back once more to thump in frustration. He caught my hand and pulled it to the side. He lifted my chin gently with his other hand and forced me to look into his eyes again. Traces of the patterns still lingered in my mind as I stared.

"I am sorry I did not tell you. I am sorry to go back on our deal. I want more than anything to have all the time in the world to love you and for you to feel the same way." His eyes went cold, and any trace of the patterns I had read before were gone. "But I will not bond you in union—not like that, not given the circumstances or under any influence. I do not want a union out of necessity. Not for either of us. Would the ends justify the means?"

He cupped my cheek even more firmly as I tried to look away. Staring into his eyes didn't just allow me to be honest with him, but with myself.

"No," I finally said.

He let go of my hand and my cheek and pushed himself off the wall.

"It doesn't change the fact that you don't get to decide for me!" I yelled after him, but he was gone.

I thumped the wall with a solid kick, but it was not as satisfying as his chest had been.

Chapter 23

BOUNDARIES

I spent the next hour wandering the open gardens of the White Cliffs. It only took five minutes for me to cool down and decide to find Denali—not to yell again, but to talk. Unfortunately, I was lost. I slung one of my six orbs into the open air over the balcony and whipped it back into my palm. I did this over and over. I needed to do something. With my emotions tempered, I knew Denali had been right to walk away. I was growing fond of him, close to him even. I knew him deeply now, but I still knew very little about him. I wasn't ready to be bound to him forever, and he knew that.

Ukaleq's words struck my mind like lightning. She had said her words were bound in heaven and earth. Did that mean a union was forever? More questions flooded my mind. How had I not thought to ask a god more? Hell, even one of her children might've been able to answer a few questions, but I had not encountered a single person in my hour of wandering. I slung the orb out a great distance in frustration.

The sound of my orb zipping through the air was a soothing reminder of training with my mentor. It helped me think. My orb slapped into my palm with a satisfying smack, and I moved to sling it out again, but I paused as the sound of whipping orbs continued.

I cocked my head and followed the sound around a bend to find a large open courtyard. In it I found Rochelle practicing forms with her orbs. I leaned up against the arched opening and watched her movements closely. She moved through the motions flawlessly. Her eyes were closed, but the orbs moved with a precision few slingers ever mastered. She froze midstep, and all of her orbs ceased moving immediately.

"Have you come for a lesson?"

The sight of her orbs stopping so abruptly and then floating in the air momentarily before dropping to the ground caused me to stand up straight.

"I'm lost," I said.

"Spar with me so I can finish my practice early, and I will guide you back to your rooms. How did your meeting with Ukaleq fare?"

The woman recalled her orbs and circled me in a manner that instinctively caused me to match. I had accepted the spar without even realizing.

"Met a reaper, saw some patterns in the spiritual realm, and Denali walked out before we could be joined in union."

"Very interesting. Maybe I should have stayed," she said.

"I doubt you'd have been much help, but I do have some questions."

"First we spar while my blood is still pumping. I'm curious to see how sloppy you all have gotten." She signaled for me to advance.

"Just fight me like a slinger—no shaman funny business."

She nodded and signaled again.

I dropped into the third Noble Form with four of my orbs on the offensive, two in reserve for defense. She dropped into the second Noble Form and whipped two of her orbs in a circular motion, batting away my four orbs with two swipes.

"Too linear," she chided.

I changed my footing and orbs to the sixth Noble Form and approached with rapid footwork. As my four orbs slung forward, I staggered them, and to make it even more interesting, I dropped one of my defensive orbs to my right foot and kicked it forward for a fifth and final shot.

Rochelle had changed to a stance I did not recognize, possibly a combination of sixth and second. It was a defensive retreat I had never seen, but it countered me effectively. The fifth and final shot she kicked back at me.

"I said no shaman funny business!"

She smiled and lifted her toe into the air, revealing an orb of her own. I was genuinely surprised, as I had never met another person who had used their feet to sling before.

My mentor had always mocked me for it, but it had come so naturally.

The sparring continued for another twenty minutes. It had been a long time since I had fought anyone competent enough for more than a fast draw duel. We were both breathing raggedly and drenched in sweat. I had tossed the robe to the ground in one of our exchanges. It was sporting a few holes now, but none of her orbs had managed to land on me. I had not landed a single on her either.

In a risky move, I dropped my last defensive orb and dropped into the sixteenth Noble Form. Rochelle smirked before I closed my eyes to concentrate. All six of my orbs slung forward. The beat in my mind drummed rapidly, and each orb moved at its own beat with its own intervals. They spun in every direction around Rochelle at the highest velocity I could muster, their movements only decipherable to me. I let my attack fly. I opened my eyes as I heard the sound of flesh piercing and blood squirting. I let out a gasp upon seeing Rochelle holding her abdomen.

"Very good," she said, smiling. "But it was a suicidal move. Maybe if you had a few orbs in reserve you could have survived. Don't worry, I'll heal right up. You may want to check your chest."

I looked down and saw one of Rochelle's orb sitting over my heart. I felt my breath catch and my stomach lurch.

"Come with me. Let's get cleaned up before I take you back to your rooms. Wouldn't want to chafe with all this sweat."

Her orb left my chest in a gust of air and flew back to her waist. I took a deep breath, grabbed my robe, and followed her.

"Yeah, chafing is the worst."

Rochelle stripped down as we walked out of the courtyard, letting her clothes lie where they fell. We walked through an arch to a spring lined with stone. Rochelle flicked her wrist, and the water began to steam.

"Let me know if it's too hot. I like it extra steamy to clear my lungs."

"You seem less abrasive today," I said.

She laughed and rubbed her forehead. "You'll have to forgive me. I was not expecting newcomers when you arrived. I forget myself sometimes when I spend too much time at the White Cliffs. It's been a few centuries. Working with my totems always helps ground me again. I'll be honest with you, though. I do want something from you. We'll get to that."

I stripped my garments and slowly descended into the heat. The steam began to collect so thick that I had to sit very close to Rochelle to see her. I caught a glimpse of her abdomen before she submerged. My orb hadn't even left a scar, but she was covered in other scars. Hundreds of them.

"Are you immortal?" I asked.

"To an extent. Not like the pirates of Aaru Bay, but I won't age, and most things can't kill me."

"But you were a slinger first," I pointed out. "So you learned to be a shaman? How old are you?"

Rochelle poured soap into the water and dipped under. She let her hair fall back over her shoulders; it had a shine to it now. I dipped my own head under quickly and marveled as I felt the scum melt right off my scalp and face. I pulled my braid over my shoulder to see it had the same dark shine as Rochelle's. The woman took a deep breath of the steam and cleared her throat.

"Quite the opposite, actually. I was a shaman first, a few millennia ago. I don't remember how many it's been now. More than twenty, I imagine."

I simply stared. It was a moment before I realized my jaw was open.

"I know," she said with a smile. "I look amazing."

"No," I said. "Well, yes. But you've been sitting up in these cliffs for more than twenty thousand years? What a waste. What are you even doing with yourself?"

"It's hard to explain. If you stay long enough, you may be able to learn."

I shook my head. "No. The world is a mess, and you people are practically gods. You sit up here ignoring it?"

Rochelle's face grew stern, her eyes sharp, and then her expression softened just as quickly. She let out a soft sigh.

"I was a shaman before the great spirits forsook the Unkubernan. Before it was the Unkubernan, it was lush and green. Some of the great spirits declared themselves gods and crowded to fill the coast against the invasion of the immortal pirates of Aaru. Other great spirits left the world entirely, like mine did. It was a chaotic time. Without any divine power and no law in the Unkubernan, I developed the martial form known as slinging and erected the Roche covenant."

"You're the first," I repeated for my own sake.

"Yes, I am the first."

"Why did you leave?" I asked.

"I was getting old, and I'd heard of a goddess to the east who had not abandoned her lands to protect the coast. That's when I found Ukaleq and some of her followers."

"Why didn't you come back and help the Unkubernan?" I asked.

"I did a few times, actually. There were many moments in history that grew particularly tumultuous and the jurisdiction of the Unkubernan came into question by other great spirits. Gods would try to enforce their policies on our people despite forsaking us, a tax the people could not afford to pay. Sometimes a slinger would declare themselves a monarch. Our oaths were sacred, but they were never enforced like yours were. Swearing a covenant on penalty of death . . . Honestly, I don't know what Slalal and Seattle were thinking."

"They probably wanted commitment. You didn't want to come back, so why would anyone else? Why did you stop coming back?" I asked.

Rochelle lingered on this question, her eyes looking out in the distance. "I don't remember. I know that I stopped believing people could follow the oaths along the way, so I stopped trying to save the order from itself. I let the order crumble. The Unkubernan went a millennia or so without any Roche slingers. They managed just fine. The great spirits learned their lessons, and the society that formed in the Unkubernan seemed stable enough. No one became strong enough to claim themselves a monarch."

"Swearing on death seemed to keep people on the straight and narrow," I commented.

"But once that was broken, few people could live up to it. Most people only became a Roche slinger for power, and then there's you. Your swear was still intact after the reckoning. What happened?"

"I swore it after." I put my hand to my chest, where the anguish had struck me so hard before, where Death's stone had hung around my neck for so many years. I did not tell her how I had sworn the oaths after my mentor had given up his life to destroy them, how I had done it to make him proud, to honor him, to feel close to him again. It felt like a lie now that I knew the truth about his true goals.

"That would have made Slalal proud. I liked him." She went silent for a moment. "You are a fool, though."

I did not quite know how to respond at first. I stammered a few syllables before my thoughts turned to a tirade. "You don't believe in the covenant? How could you not? Didn't you make it?"

She had a glass in her hand that I had not noticed. She took a deep drink from it and let out a crisp sigh. "That I did. I built it to keep people in line. We needed law and order, but nobody could figure out how to be civilized in all the chaos."

I was leaning in closer now, hanging on every word she spoke of my people's history. I found a drink bumping the back of my arm. I could not tell if it was floating on the water's surface or in the air, but I accepted it and took a deep drink as I had seen Rochelle do. It went down smooth, and the effects were immediate. I eased back and leaned against the stone wall, allowing myself to submerge all the way to my chin, waiting for more of Rochelle's tale.

"After so many millennia, I don't enjoy telling the story anymore," she said. I sat upright in protest, but she cut me off before I could get a word in. "Let's talk about your problems instead. You said you had questions. I have my own. Why did Denali walk away? It's the only way to save his life. You know of Pahokute's curse?"

"I only know that Denali is sick. I don't know how the curse works."

"It's a wicked thing, but it's not too different from your oaths sworn on Death's stone. Denali swore to his god in servitude, and the price is the vitality in his organs. It's very concerning, actually—not just for Denali, but what Pahokute is doing with the results of the trade. I shiver to think . . ." Rochelle paused as she noticed my head cocked and a hundred questions on the tip of my tongue. "Oh, that's right. You wouldn't know anything about shamanism or the great spirits. I'm talking over you, aren't I? Never mind all that. You probably want to know why Ukaleq could break your curse and not his, yes? She is known as the bond breaker for slingers who swore their oaths on Death's stone for the last few centuries, but she does so by negotiating with the reapers. They are more than happy to relinquish the oaths; they despise them, in fact. But a curse by another great spirit? Those trades do not come so easily."

"I'm sorry. Centuries?" I asked. "You said my mentor and Seattle were the ones to start people swearing the covenant on Death's stone."

"Yes, a few centuries ago. They were slingers who found their way to Ukaleq, two young brothers chasing adventure and glory. My order had been dismantled millennia before, but those boys had grown up romanticizing the stories of noble slingers bringing justice to a lawless godforsaken land. So when they found Ukaleq, they both chose to leave and start the order again, with their extreme little twist."

I stared off into the steam, which obscured anything around the stone spring. The drink in my hand was empty now, and another floated toward me. I tossed my empty glass into the water and gladly took the next. Slalal never told me he had been the one to restart the order, or that he was centuries old, or that he had already met Ukaleq himself.

"Was he a shaman too?" I asked.

"Slalal? No. Like Seattle, he was just a very good slinger. They learned a few tricks that suited them while they were here, but they didn't have the patience to become full shamans."

"Seattle's boulder, is that because of Ukaleq's power?" I asked.

"You know, I never quite puzzled those boulders out. I would assume Ukaleq's blessing granted them the ability. There would be no other way to sling something with that kind of mass. You'd rip yourself apart."

The amusement in her voice at the notion chilled me despite the hot water and steam.

"Who did Slalal join in union? That is Ukaleq's policy, right? But he never mentioned a wife."

"The brothers sealed themselves to each other."

The disgusted look on my face must have tipped Rochelle off to the fact that I knew nothing about the union.

"The union is not a sexual one. No wonder Denali walked away in the heat of the moment. You don't know the first thing about unions. Do you know why Ukaleq demands a union in order to grant her blessing to an individual?" She waited for me to shake my head. "Raw power consumes. It's a universal law, like gravity or death. In the case of us mortals, it is true on two fronts, both mental and physical. Ukaleq's blessing is different than other gods' in that she does not inflict her will upon us. We maintain free agency even when we use her power, her authority. Other gods enact agency as a mental tax. The fact that Denali still has so much of his own will and personality after serving a god for a few centuries is a testament to his character. That's what shamans use their totems for, to keep themselves grounded and not lose their sense of self."

My head was cocked again, trying to follow.

"Sorry, I'm trying to be plain. My point is, Ukaleq does not inflict her will on us. Her power is free to us, but it is still possible to draw too much. She does not imply the mental tax, but the physical tax is an impossible trade-off. It is possible to burn yourself out and never be able to access that power again. So do you see why she requires us to join in unions?"

"No," I replied honestly.

Rochelle took another long drink before continuing.

"When you receive her blessing in a union, you can't burn out on that physical tax. If you draw in too much power, the burden is shared between the two. This way the power cannot consume you on a physical level. You just reach a limit. It's a dampening effect."

"So shamans under Ukaleq can't become soulless," I said.

"Exactly." She nodded.

"Well, why didn't you lead with that?"

"Context, dear," she said with a sigh.

"Okay, so that explains the physical. How does a union protect you mentally?" I asked.

"Relationship. Pure and simple. Centuries can be maddening if you live only for yourself or for a cause. Relationships require humility and cooperation."

"Are these unions eternal?" I asked.

"Very good." She smiled an almost wicked smile. "Ukaleq's words bind in heaven and earth."

"Okay," I said. "So let's say I bond Denali and find out I can't stand him."

"Oh, it's almost certain. It comes and goes, but binding your soul to another is not something most mortals get an opportunity to do. No matter who you bind yourself to, you're better off being bound to somebody in eternity."

"So you think I should do it."

"That's my motivation in spending time with you right now. I want you to bond Denali. Not to save him, necessarily. Live or die, it means nothing to me. I want you bound to him so your oath is broken and you focus on your relationship. I want you to give up your quest."

"Excuse me?" I clutched at the anguish of my broken bonds. She had no idea they were already gone.

"I am tired of the Roche slingers," she explained. "It is an experiment that has run its course, and it has failed time and time again. Slalal and Seattle proved that even upon the penalty of death, mortals cannot live up to the ideals." The air around us was growing heavy. Her eyes seemed darker. "Like I said, you are a fool. I saw how much you clung to the creed. I don't want you to go back out there and keep it alive. It is far past time for it to die. I do not want my name associated with the idea for another twenty millennia."

She took another drink and slammed it across the stone outside the spring. I could hear the cup shatter through the camouflage of the steam, but with the crash the air grew less heavy, and Rochelle's face softened. She simply watched me now.

"Well?" she asked.

Even without my oaths, I thought to myself. "I really am the last slinger of Roche," I whispered.

I stood up out of the water and looked down to Rochelle.

"Tell me, Rochelle." It did not sound like my voice. It was harder. "If I bond Denali and give up on my oaths, will I turn into the same callous monster as you in a millennia or two?"

"Impudent child," she sneered.

"Impudent? I call it like I see it. You may have had good intentions once upon a time, but look at you now. You sit up here and ignore the slaughter of entire towns because you can't fix everything in one go and walk away? Do you really believe mortals are the problem with an unjust world? What alternative do they have? The gods abandoned them, and now you want to as well? The creed hasn't failed. You have."

I marched out of the spring, causing the water to churn around me. I grabbed my garments and hurriedly flung my robe over my shoulders. Before I could get my arms in, I felt something smack me in the back hard enough to send me flying forward in a tumble.

I pushed myself to my feet and turned to face her as I donned my hole-ridden robe. I did my best not to wince at the bruise that was now forming across my back. She stood there naked out of the water, looking no less threatening as she fumed. I took solace in the fact that she was not allowed to kill me while I was in the White Cliffs.

"Get your ego in check, you old crone. Change your damn name if you have to, but don't tell me how to live my life."

I turned and walked away. I still was not sure how to find my room or Denali. It dawned on me that while she was not allowed to kill me, she could still torture me if it suited her.

"You sound just like him!" she called after me. My heart raced even faster. "Seattle says the same things you say! He wasn't always a murderer! The fight for justice turns to a fight to rule, which turns to a fight to conquer! It always ends the same! You know nothing, child!"

I walked until the sound of her voice faded, then I kept walking to put as much distance between us as possible.

CHAPTER 24

TOUCH

I never found my room. I was not even certain which level of the White Cliffs it was on. I slept on a bench over an open veranda that night. I was used to roughing it, and the weather never seemed to run sour here. I awoke to the sound of voices as small groups of people streamed by. I sat up to see Denali rushing over to me.

"Amarantha! There you are. I have been looking for you all night."

It put a smile on my face to see his concern and to know that he had looked for me, but then I felt the guilt.

"You shouldn't be putting that kind of stress on yourself," I said.

"No need to start. I will be fine."

He did, in fact, look fine as he clutched his staff. It was noticeably skinnier than before.

"Is that keeping you alive?" I asked.

He shrugged. "We need to get moving."

"Why? What's happening?"

He looked over to the stream of people. "From what I gather, Ukaleq has requested an audience with everyone. Everyone is speculating that it is concerning Seattle."

"A trial?" I jumped to my feet, and we filed into the crowd together.

"No, I do not believe so. They do not do that sort of thing here. Ukaleq does not hold people accountable for their past sins."

The hop in my step quickly turned to a march. I kept my pace, but I was less enthusiastic than before.

The hall we entered was large enough to house thousands of people in a circular terrace that overlooked a center stage. It was a full house. Yamak and Rochelle were down near the stage. Yamak saw us enter and rushed up to meet us.

"This way please." He gestured for us to follow.

He deposited us in the front row and made to leave us there.

"Are we on trial?" I asked as the man scurried away without answering.

"I guess we will have to wait and see." Denali smiled at me.

"Ugh, you know I hate that answer." His smile grew

even broader as he nodded gleefully. "Don't take pleasure in my torture, Denali."

Rochelle led Seattle and Tokala onto the stage. Tokala gave me a small wave, which I awkwardly returned, but Seattle ignored us entirely. He seemed solemn, almost nervous, as he inspected the room. Everyone in the chamber fell silent as a darkness filled the sky above. Ukaleq's figure began to form before us on the stage. Everyone rose to their feet, and Denali and I followed suit. Denali bowed his head along with the other people in the audience. Even Tokala and Seattle dipped their heads slightly. I watched.

"Thank you for coming, my children," the goddess began. "I have asked you all here to counsel. There is a sickness among us that even I do not understand. It must be addressed, and it must not be allowed to spread."

Seattle lurched, then lifted off the ground. He was being held still in the air.

"I ask you all to bear witness to this intervention. I do not detain Seattle as punishment or retribution. He is contaminated by something not of this world. All must be inspected."

The room flashed, and I watched my body drop to the floor. I saw the blackness dripping from Seattle's luminous form. It had been disturbing to witness when I had first encountered it in the spiritual realm with the ayahuasca, but it had not occurred to me that it might be some sort of spiritual contagion. I instinctively tried shut my eyes, careful not to look at the goddess again in fear that I might get lost in her eternal patterns, but I was reminded that I did not have eyes to close while in this form. I looked down and reached for Denali's hand. He clasped tightly as

I looked to see our luminous hands slowly fuse into one. The patterns swirled into each other as we touched. This had not happened the last time we were luminous in the spiritual realm before the goddess.

In that moment, I felt all of him. I experienced every emotion and every thought of his that bubbled to the surface. His never-ending eyes grew wider, and the patterns that made up his luminous jaw dropped open as he gaped at me. I felt the shock and embarrassment surge through him; it made me want to pull away as if I had done something wrong, but he clasped even tighter. A strong sense of appreciation overwhelmed me.

"I apologize for my shocked reaction. I forget you are not familiar with the ways of shamans."

His voice was in my head. I looked around to see if anyone else could hear, but nobody was paying any attention to us as Ukaleq swept through the room examining each individual in attendance one by one.

"Can you hear my thoughts as well?"

He nodded. *"Emotions and thoughts we have will be unavoidable as we clasp together. This is usually reserved for spiritual . . . bonding. Behind closed doors."*

I could feel embarrassment rise in him as he shifted a little and looked around. I could not help the chortle that erupted from me. He smiled and shrugged in return.

"I must apologize though." A deeper sense of embarrassment arose. No, it was shame. *"I can see deeper than the surface. Deeper than you probably want me to see."*

"What do you see?" I pressed.

"You are stubborn. You are scared to be left alone. Your self-esteem has been shattered over and over again. Each time you have been

abandoned or left alone, you have been broken down to nothing. It has destroyed you repeatedly."

My eyes felt like they were going to bulge out of my head, but I remembered I was a luminous being and not flesh and blood. He likely could not see my full expression, but he could feel what I was feeling as I faced the truth in his words. He was reading my soul and bearing it at my feet. I did not know what to do. I wanted to justify the feelings to him. I wanted to hide. A part of me even wanted to die.

"But." He stopped me. *"Each time you get back up. Each time you are broken, your principles come back stronger. You have mended yourself back together so many times that your morals are resolute. Your sense of obligation to justice, well, it is like nothing I have ever seen before. You light a fire in my soul."*

My fears melted. This man saw me clearer than I was usually willing to see myself, and he did not look away. No, he found reasons to look deeper, to see more, and to love. I felt the emotion rise stronger than anything had up until this point. It occurred to me that the feeling had been sitting there the whole time, as though it had been radiating from him like warmth radiates from a stone at the end of a hot day. Except now the heat was impossible to ignore, as though the stone had rolled out of a hot fire.

He looked around to check how far Ukaleq had gotten with her inspection.

"We still have some time. I feel bad, as you can tell, that I looked. But to make it fair, you are welcome to take a deeper look at me."

"Is this a ploy to make me fall in love with you?"

"I'm not entirely sure what you will see." He shrugged. *"If I wanted to trick you into a union, I would have done it earlier. You know how I feel about the situation."*

I looked at the darker swirls around some of his organs, which tarnished his luminous form. The curse that should have killed him by now still weighed over us.

"Will it be like before? Will I go too deep and risk getting stuck?"

He shook his luminous head.

"Before you studied patterns visually. This is a different sense. It is physical like touch, but you experience what I feel. Visual patterns are dangerous because the mind cannot understand without training or guidance, but the body can feel something temporarily."

I reached into him with our clasped hands and tried to feel. It came quite easily. It felt like I was reaching into him through our fused hands. I could feel some of the patterns I had read before as I reached around. This felt much more invasive than reading patterns had. I could feel his sense of curiosity, the joy he experienced from his enthusiasm. These truths were constants. They were almost always there, but there was something else there, something behind those truths. There was a fire burning behind them. I wanted to reach out and discover what the fire was, but I feared being burned.

"Go ahead. Nothing will hurt you."

I reached out and touched the fire. It was a specific insecurity. As I reached around, I could tell just how hot this fire had burned in the past. There was something to the texture surrounding this flame that spoke to me. The flame burned almost to a point of pure consumption at times, times in his life when there had been no guidance. Denali had put so much faith in others and in gods that when that guidance had dried up, his insecurity burned. It was masked only by his curiosity and enthusiasm to an obsessive degree.

Something had put out these flames. I needed to find what could possibly have doused the insecurity that had raged. I reached around until I splashed into something. I felt water trickle down into a well. As I touched the trickling water, I felt the source. Wisdom spurned on by curiosity and trial and error was the source. I felt myself smile at the perfect circle of Denali's conflict and resolution in his own nature. I reached down and touched the water in the well and realized it was different somehow.

The well was fed by wisdom until it overflowed, but it was not the only source of water, nor was it the true nature of the well. I reached down into the well and felt patience. His patience was overwhelming. I could not feel the bottom of the well. It seemed like it might go on forever.

I pulled back, and our hands nearly broke apart from their intertwined patterns.

"What did you feel?" he asked hesitantly.

We both looked over to see Ukaleq finishing her examinations.

"Your struggles with faith and guidance, your fear of making the wrong decisions, and how you masked them with obsessive curiosity and enthusiasm." He shrugged in a way I was coming to expect from him. *"But I also saw how you overcame that insecurity with wisdom, and in doing so you have an unfathomable capacity for patience."*

"That could have gone worse, I suppose." He fidgeted his shoulders a little.

"I've seen enough to know," I said.

"To know what?" he asked.

"To know that if I look again, no matter what I see or feel, I can trust you."

I felt myself take a deep breath and let it out slowly. I looked down and saw that it was my body lying on the floor that had taken the deep breath.

"It feels like it has been a long time since you trusted someone," he said.

"It really has."

"You are all clean of this unknown infestation." Ukaleq's voice spread throughout the room.

Just as quickly as we had been forced into the spiritual realm, I opened my eyes from my body on the floor and took a quick breath. I looked up and saw that Denali had been leaning against his totem the entire time. I envied that ability as I pushed myself from the stone. He reached down to help me up. As our fingers touched, I could almost feel him the way I had before. The sensation had been just as real as any of my physical senses, but so different. I could not stop myself from grinning at the thought of it as he pulled me to my feet. Ukaleq drew our attention again as she began to speak. I felt heat in my cheeks as I realized I was fawning over a man as a literal goddess was manifesting herself before me.

"Only Seattle must be quarantined," she said.

"This is outrageous!" he screamed as he hovered in the air, detained by the goddess.

His voice was still grim even as it elevated. His protests came more as a boom in the stadium than an elevated scream.

"I'm not contagious," he continued. "Calling it quarantine does not change the fact that you are imprisoning me!"

"Your condition must be studied. Once the threat of danger has been eliminated, you will be freed," the goddess said.

"You said it yourself: I am not free to go. Therefore, I am a prisoner. If it is to be a quarantine and not imprisonment, then it must be voluntary. I do not volunteer it for the safety of others."

The goddess shook her head. "Then this sickness has infected your capacity, and you are under my jurisdiction for care. Do any besides the afflicted object?"

The room was silent. Seattle looked to Tokala with a seething expression. She crossed her arms and looked away. Ukaleq's form began to fade, and sunlight began to flood from overhead again. Seattle floated out of the chamber, though he visibly struggled against it.

The broad smile across Tokala's face rivaled the length of the perpendicular scar. Her smile was contagious as she looked to me. It did not feel awkward to share a smile with her in that moment. We both felt the freedom and were reveling in it. I did not know for sure if Seattle was permanently dealt with, but it was progress, and I now had someone next to me that I trusted. I gave Denali's hand a tight squeeze as I realized I was still holding it.

COMMITMENTS

I awoke that evening from a sleep so deep and restful that my body had gone stiff but at the same time felt refreshed. I grabbed a fresh robe and plucked a mint bristle from the bedside to chew on. I exited the bed chambers and looked around for Denali. He had been the one to suggest resting after the morning's revelations. He had assured me that I would sleep well, and he had not been wrong.

"You're still out here? Shouldn't you be resting as well?" I asked.

"I do not know." He forced a weak smile for me.

I squinted my eyes to inspect him closely. "How do you mean?"

"I do not understand this curse. All I know is that my organs start to fail. I heal them, and then I am fine for a while."

"But the union would for sure fix it?" I asked.

He nodded slowly.

"Then let's do it," I stated plainly.

"Amarantha, unions are not to be taken lightly."

"And neither is a life." I pointed my finger into his chest. "Especially not yours. You are the only ally I have left."

"Unions are a deeper connection than anything you have experienced. I cannot . . ."

He trailed off as I raised my pointing finger to his eye level, but I cupped his clean-shaven face instead. "You're not forcing anything on me. I've given it a lot of thought."

"That is what I am worried about. Would this even be a point of conversation if I were not dying?"

"Probably not." I let my hand fall and shrugged. "But I'm glad it is."

He cocked his head appraisingly.

"As you can imagine," I said with a smirk, "I'm not a philosopher like you. I've spent the majority of my life surviving or hiding. Romance is foreign to me, and sex is a distraction." His cheeks flushed slightly. "I'm glad I've had a chance to think about it. I am done running. I don't want to be giving it thought too late. I trust you, Denali. I can't say I love you—I don't know what that means—but I've been thinking about what Rochelle said."

His face grew dark and sour. He was clearly still disturbed by my account. "You should not dwell on that woman's words."

"I don't need to agree with her to find my own wisdom," I pointed out.

Denali blinked hard and refocused his eyes. "You are absolutely right. You may become a philosopher yet."

He smiled at me, and I returned my own smile as I soaked in the praise before continuing.

"She said Seattle and my mentor joined each other in union. They were brothers. It didn't have to be romantic. Most of the shamans here get bored of each other after a few centuries, but they are still in their unions. The union can be a tool just as much as it can be anything else."

Denali's sour face returned as he sucked in one of his cheeks until his lips formed a crooked purse. He slowly started to nod and then shook his head in disagreement.

"No, I do not want that." He reached down and grabbed both my hands. "Amarantha, I am not afraid to die, and I do not want to abandon you, but if we go through with this, I will never stop wanting to experience the world with you. To change the world with you. I do not just believe that you will become that sketch I made of you. I know it, and I want to support you. Forever."

The sensation of the flame and the well became real again in each hand he held. In one hand I felt his desire for guidance burning. In the other I felt the deep well of patience.

"My principles are my own. I can't lead you," I warned him.

"I know. I am done taking orders. I am ready to live on my own terms, but I do not want to do it alone."

I smiled and leaned in to kiss him. He was apprehensive at first, but then he relaxed. He let go of my hands and reached around my waist to pull me in close. He was only slightly taller than me, but his arms fit perfectly around my lower back. Our lips moved slowly and in sync as though riding the same wave. I felt his breath caress my cheek as he moved lower and began kissing more aggressively just below my jaw toward my neck. I lifted my chin to bare it for him, and he passionately attacked it.

Like mating birds in the sky, we moved rapidly to undress each other, but we never collided. We deftly performed high-speed maneuvers as we undressed and moved to the bed.

That night I felt more than the physical demands of sex or the awkward moments shared between strangers. I trusted him completely, I was ready for him, I wanted him, and I felt pleasures I had never known before.

PARTNERS

Denali and I held hands facing each other in front of the goddess, just the three of us. This was in part because there was no one else to attend. The only Children of Ukaleq, what the shamans here called themselves, who had actually taken time to introduce themselves to us were Yamak and Rochelle. The pair had left on a research mission into the origins of Seattle's blackened soul. I had not spoken with Rochelle since our last encounter anyway. Millennia-old women might not hold grudges, but I still needed my space from her.

I took a deep breath to quell the fluttering in my stomach. I kept reminding myself that this boiled down to a platonic partnership. Even if it was an eternal partnership, it was for mutual benefit—never mind that we were now sleeping together or that we played so well together in bed. The fluttering started again.

I looked into Denali's eyes as the goddess broke his bonds to Pahokute by claiming him as her child and granting her blessing. I could feel the genuine trust in his expression. Being able to trust each other was all that mattered right now.

The goddess only remained long enough to take his bond and seal us. I could not remember the words, but the desire to have them written down became an urgent knocking at the forefront of my mind. I hushed it away to focus on Denali. The goddess whisked herself away after explaining that she was needed elsewhere.

I looked to Denali's abdomen, where the image of his sickened organs still resonated in my mind.

"Is it gone?" I asked him.

He took a deep breath and held it before a grin began to creep across his face.

"It will take some time to recover, but the curse is gone."

I let out a sigh and embraced him. He held me tight and began to sniffle. I pulled back to look and saw tears.

"What's wrong?"

He smiled and inhaled sharply. "Nothing! I do not recall ever having been so happy. I was not sure anything like this was meant for me in this life."

"That reminds me. What exactly does eternal mean in this context?"

His smile faded, and his tears stopped as he looked at me with a grave expression before it quickly changed to realization and shock in his eyes.

"My gods, Amarantha. Please tell me you know about the reincarnation cycle. I forget what it means sometimes that you grew up in the Unkubernan without shamans."

"Well, no. I get the concept of reincarnation—I pay enough attention to have picked up on that—but what does it mean that you and I are eternal partners?"

He gestured for me to sit on one of the stone benches. It was hard but fortunately warm from basking in the sun.

"I sincerely hope that you do not learn something about this union and hate me for it someday."

"Is there anything I should be worried about?" I asked.

"Not that I can think of." He put his hand to his chest in exaggeration. "But you may have a different take on things as you learn." He leaned back and looked to the clouds overhead for a moment before looking back to me. "To answer your question, you have to understand our spirits. We are no different from the great spirits that govern the land, except we have bodies. When we die, our spirits learn and grow from our experiences here on Earth, so it's a cycle until one day our spirits are grand enough to act as the great spirits do here."

"So my spirit is stuck with your spirit for eternity somehow," I recapped.

"Yes. When Ukaleq says her words are bound in heaven and earth, she means that literally. Not many great spirits have that power. She might be the only one. I wonder if she's close to becoming a creator herself."

I thumped him on the shoulder to let him know he was losing me.

"Right, sorry," he said as he rubbed his shoulder. "As you can imagine, this partnership of our spirits affects us in the reincarnation cycle as well. If we die, we will find each other in the next life somehow, though I am fuzzy on timing and logistics. I will need to do some research and see if I can find one of these shamans to explain it to me."

"Children of Ukaleq," I corrected him.

"I am not using that in a sentence unless I have to." He smiled.

"Well, partner," I said as I got to my feet. "Shall we retire?"

"It's still early," he said, grinning as he took my hand.

"I think you know what I mean," I said with a mischievous smile.

As we exited the hall to the hallway overlooking the valley, we found Tokala waiting for us. Her back was to us as she faced the majesty of the valley, only she was not looking to the valley; she was staring at her feet.

"Tokala?" I asked.

She turned and looked up to see us.

"Oh, hello," she said, but her expression was distant.

"Can we help you with something?"

She snapped out of it and looked me in the eye.

"If you are hungry, the other Children of Ukaleq requested you join us for lunch."

Denali and I shared a look. He wore a sideways grin and shrugged.

"Lead on," I said.

Tokala was quiet for the entire descent. I held Denali's thick arm as we traversed the halls and descended multiple flights. I began to smell cooked meat, and my mouth watered immediately. Eating nothing but fruit for the last few days had been doing a number on my regularity.

"Beben cooked up some of his stock for the occasion," Tokala said as we approached a courtyard.

"On our behalf?"

Tokala nodded.

"You're both Ukaleq's children now. Most everyone was very sweet to me once Seattle and I were sealed. Even after he was . . . well, you know."

"Right," I said.

I did not know how to respond. She was just as happy as I was that he was locked up, but something was clearly bothering her. My concern for Tokala vanished as the hum of conversation reached my ears. We turned to enter the courtyard and were greeted by the applause of hundreds of shamans.

They were a livelier bunch than I had anticipated. My dealings with Yamak and Rochelle must have soured my outlook, even after witnessing some of their revelries. Nobody here seemed to be the coldhearted philosophers I had expected. Lunch turned to festivities of music, dance, and alcohol. Tokala and a few others were incapacitated from the alcohol by supper, but the festivities bled into the evening.

The fluttering in my stomach returned occasionally, but it was not nerves; it was excitement. The world felt full of new possibilities, and the jovial festivities in our honor made the day feel even more special. It framed the union Denali and I had just entered with enthusiasm I had been denying myself before.

Two of the shamans were performing a skit on stage that left us all laughing. I looked to Denali as the sun began to set behind us and squeezed his hand. He took a moment to catch his breath from the laughter and wiped his eyes dry before looking at me. I bit my lip to hold back my own smile at seeing him laugh so hard. I did not know this kind of joy was left for me to find in the world, and it was not the alcohol talking. I leaned in close to whisper in his ear.

"I think I can love you," I said.

He pulled back and looked me in the eyes, studying me.

"You, my love, are the fire in my soul." He wrapped his arm around me and pulled me in closer.

CHAPTER 27

CONCERNS

The scent of rain filled my nostrils as I paced through my new training regimen on the balcony. I watched the goddess roll dark clouds into the valley. I could not actually see her in any form, but I had been told she controlled the weather, as did most great spirits in their region of authority.

The concept was becoming less foreign to me now that Denali had been training me. I was beginning to understand how it took shamans a few lifetimes to master some of the abilities. My new training regimen had expanded from working with my totems in practicing the Noble Forms to now include the shamanic manipulations. Denali had broken them down into divination, enhancement, transmission, and transmutation. He had said they grew increasingly complex, but understanding these four principles would build a firm foundation.

I was stuck on the concept of divination, simply communicating with the spirit of an object and such. When he had explained it, I thought I would be a natural given my affinity for making totems, but I had been wrong. I had a stone from the garden before me. The stone was within Ukaleq's jurisdiction, so she had complete authority over it, which meant I had complete authority over it. But when I tugged on my connection to the stone, nothing happened. My connection through Ukaleq's authority felt different. I could not feel it out the way I had expected to.

I huffed and moved on from trying to understand the connection and began attempting to communicate through that connection using divination.

"Hello, rock," I said through my connection to it.

There was no response.

"How are you today?"

Again, no response. I let my frustration into the connection and felt the sentiment push right back up the connection into my finger.

"Fascinating," I said, allowing the emotion to move through the connection as well.

I felt arrogance resonate back through to me, and I could've almost sworn I heard the stone say, "Yes, I am."

It was a breakthrough.

Time to attempt enhancement.

"Be a flat river stone," I said without understanding how to convey any emotion in the demand.

"Go away."

I jumped back at the clear order the rock had just barked at me. I picked up the rock to chuck it into the fountain, but it felt wrong. The rock had wishes, and it no longer felt right to chuck it aside. I was confused. I placed it under a tree that still had red leaves instead.

I walked back over to my bench on the balcony. The rain clouds were getting closer, but it was a nice enough morning that I did not care. I tugged on my connection to one of my orbs at my hip and caught it in my palm. This connection I understood. Divination felt like a one-way street with totems. My spirit and the totems spirit were in unison. This made enhancement easier. I asked the orb to lie flat, and it squished itself across my palm. I asked it to soften, and it became malleable in my fingers. I asked it to warm up, and it warmed my hand until it was almost too hot to hold. Then I asked it to return to its previous form as my orb and hover. It obeyed. I had seen Slalal do it many times and had always thought he compressed his connection so tightly, like how I coiled them to my hip, that the totems stood up on that connection. Now I could see what he had really been doing.

I let the soft drizzle from the goddess envelop me. The leaves in the valley below were displaying different shades of yellow, orange, and red, and the morning air was crisp. Denali had explained this to be the autumn season, but he did not think we would actually get snow. I was a little disappointed. We were high enough that there should have been snow naturally.

"That is some early training. Nightmares again? Or are you preparing for something?" Denali said as he kissed my cheek from behind and placed a pastry in my hand.

I was growing far too accustomed to these delicacies. Once the Children of Ukaleq had accepted us, they showered us with gifts, and our standard of living increased drastically. We were happy. Bringing up my concerns always felt like a blemish on that happiness, but Denali did not seem to mind.

"I'm just worried about Roca, I suppose, and Tokala too. She stopped showing up for our walks, and she seemed so quiet and down last month."

Denali made himself comfortable on a stone bench before responding. "I did not realize you two had gotten so close."

"Well, we were starting to. Despite our bad blood in the past, we have a lot in common. I haven't been able to find her recently, even when I try to hunt her down."

Denali shrugged. "I am not certain how to help you with Tokala. I ran into Beben and Kalaku while fetching these pastries, and they invited us to join them for dinner this evening. Maybe that will get your mind off of Roca. We can even extend the invitation to Tokala if we can find the woman. They may have some herbs that could help distract you as well, or cheer Tokala up if she really is in a rough patch."

"I don't want to medicate my problems away. The people here are too soft."

"Are they not your people now?" he asked.

"That would imply I want to be like them. Do you?"

He shrugged and took a bite of his pastry.

"I could spend many lifetimes here just learning. I have already learned more in the last few months than I had in a century back home." He paused and took another bite of his pastry. "But learning and living are two very different things."

"Exactly. We need to get back in the world at some point." I recalled my six orbs to my belt. In all these months I had not made more. I stuck to the six my mentor had required of us.

"Is that what you are training for? You will not become a great shaman in a few months. It can take years—even decades—to learn the basics."

"I'm in no hurry to be a shaman; that's what I have you for. I don't want to stay here for too long," I explained.

"How long do we stay for?" he asked. "Until you have figured out how to work your boulder?"

I smiled and put my finger to his chest. "You're changing the topic to distract me." I sauntered over to the bench near the fountain. "Besides, I already have."

He froze with his mouth open, pastry in hand, then let his hand fall.

"When did this happen? Today?"

I nodded excitedly.

"How? What did it take? Was it the transfiguration we discussed? Does it require anchoring yourself?"

"It's even simpler than all that."

I could not contain my excitement watching Denali struggle to work it out.

"Will you please enlighten me?" Exasperation spilled from him.

"Fine," I said with a little more squeak in my voice than I had intended. "We slingers use our connection to our totems like a thread. The stronger your connection to the orb, the tighter that thread. It's less elastic, so the stronger that connection, the faster the orb moves when you pull on it or whip it. You get the basics, right? We just do it at a precision that takes years of training."

"Oh, yes. I have been practicing." He whipped his hand, and an orb from his belt flung forward and bounced off the wall. "How does it work on the boulder though? I can move this because it's tiny. If I tried to sling something heavy, my hand would not move."

"That's why you don't sling it." I took satisfaction from his blank expression. "Do you remember how I stopped all of Yuma's orbs?"

He scratched at his chin. "Come to think of it, at the time I assumed you were just that fast and accurate, but nobody's senses are that fast."

"I can sling faster than Yuma could, so I got my orbs there in time, but you're right. There was no way for me to accurately sling against orbs I couldn't follow with my own eyes."

"So how did your orbs find their targets?" he asked.

"I asked them to," I said, fighting back a smile at his confusion. "It's an advanced technique my mentor taught me only a few months before he died. We have authority over our totems, yeah? You even said that shamans use totems to maintain their free will when channeling their great spirit's authority, and slingers use their authority to push and pull on connections from a distance. But when you make something your totem, you are developing your own authority over it."

He had one arm crossed under the other and held his own orb in front of him to study.

"How can you be sure you figured it out?" he mused, then stood and shrugged. "Don't get me wrong, I believe you. It just should not work."

"I haven't called the boulder yet. I'm not confident I won't drop it on someone by accident. But look."

I held out one of my orbs and closed my eyes to eliminate distraction, then began expressing my authority over it. I could feel it climb slowly into the air. I asked it to spin for me as it floated in place. When I opened my eyes, Denali was standing close to it. He poked it and watched it slide through the air, weightless.

"That is not possible," he said.

"Why not?" I whisked the orb back. "It's clearly doing it."

"Well, look." He displayed the orb in his palm for me. "I have authority over my orb. Even without the goddess, I can manipulate it on a fundamental level—chemically, structurally—all because I have authority over this totem." As he said this, the orb glowed and then turned to sand before turning back to his orb. "The further from reality I go in my requests to the orb, the more authority it takes—authority I do not have. I cannot break universal laws without the authority of a great spirit, and even their authority has limits. I can make this orb heavy, for example, but I cannot change the density of this orb until it crushes through the planet's core. So you are not making it weightless; you are defying gravity, friction, momentum, thrust. I do not understand it."

"And I don't understand what you just said." I shrugged and let my hands clap down to my hips. "That's my problem with this place."

"You will catch up. Many of the shamans here were slingers first or spouses of either slingers or shamans. They had no training, and they are doing fine. You will get there."

"That's not my point. I don't want to learn to do things their way. They are soft here. They are all pursuing the same thing, and nobody is living life. They don't care what happens outside these cliffs, and none of them in all their infinite wisdom can control an orb like I can—not even Rochelle."

He nodded slowly. "Yes, they lack innovation." He pumped a fist into an open palm. "The world is ours to explore. Where shall we go first?"

He pointed to a map on a table we had been studying together, shielded from the drizzle by an overhang. I hurried over to it, and he followed with a broad smile.

"The towers of Atka, the falls of Menma, or the isle kingdom of Crystallis. I want to see it all." The daydreams we had been sharing were tantalizing. There were so many different lives we could live and different adventures we could pursue someday. His excitement was contagious, and my curiosity was already piqued, but I was not ready yet. I rubbed the back of my arm as I studied the map, and my eyes were drawn back to the Unkubernan.

"I can't leave yet. The Unkubernan, that is. I need to know the people of Roca are doing well at least. I need to put my mind at ease."

"It would be a ten-day detour at the very least to check on them, but that is not my concern."

"What is?" I asked.

"Well, are they ever really going to be safe?" He began

pacing between the fountain and the map table. "If we go check on them and find danger, we get rid of it, but what about next month? We will find ourselves cleansing all the gangs out of the Unkubernan for the next thousand years before we throw our hands up like Rochelle and the rest of them here. I am not saying I do not want to help people, but I want to live a life with you too. I have spent the last two hundred years fighting wars, and I would like a few years to live life with you. The problems of the Unkubernan and all the other lands will still be here when we return." His words had sped up as he continued, and he began pacing even faster.

I leaned down to the fountain and took a sip of water to clear my dry mouth. I felt a small pit in my stomach that the cool water did not cure.

"What if we want a family?" he asked.

My cheeks warmed, and I hurried to lean back down for another gulp from the fountain. I ignored his comment about a family for now.

"When I asked about Roca, I wasn't looking for a fight," I finally said.

"Oh, gods no, Amarantha. We are both nervous talking about this. Just look at my hands." He held a palm forward to show the sweat and moved right back to pacing. "This is not a fight. We are both trying to figure out how to communicate and not offend each other. I am a wreck here trying to let you know my concern without having you think less of me."

I could not help but smile as I walked over to the strong-armed man to hold his sweaty palms in mine. "I hear you, and I agree."

"You do? I thought you would want to fix the Unkubernan or restart the Roche order or something."

"How long have you been holding that in? We can trust each other, remember? That last one is not a bad idea, even if just to do it in spite of Rochelle," I sneered. "I don't know how to solve the problems the Unkubernan faces, and I don't want to become Seattle trying to figure it out. So let's leave the White Cliffs and the Unkubernan for now. I just need to know Roca is safe before we go. So if it's at all possible, could we get there faster, like tonight? General?"

I quickly turned back to the bench I had been sitting on. My movements became rigid as I realized how intently he was watching me move.

"I apologize. I suppose I have been ruminating on this. I do not want you to feel the same way about Roca." He paused to mull it over in his mind. "Seattle's chains are holding. He will not escape the goddess until they fix his derangement."

"But we don't know what his henchmen have been up to," I explained. "The sooner we can check, the better. This gnawing feeling in my stomach has been getting worse."

Denali let out a deep sigh. I could not tell if it was relief, resignation, or perhaps both. "I understand. I have a trick I have been meaning to try now that I have the goddess's authority, but I will need to go alone to do it, and I am really going to miss you."

He pulled me in and squeezed my lower back to hold me tight. I let my knees give way slightly so he would hold me even tighter. Even with the authority of the goddess and the soft comforts of the White Cliffs, there was nothing quite as comforting as his tight embrace.

CHAPTER 28

MANIFEST

The next morning we said our farewells, and Denali launched himself into the air, staff and orbs in hand. He had explained how flying was not possible for the same reason my boulder was not possible, but he had seen Children of Ukaleq in the wild perform such feats as catapulting and controlled landings. I shushed him when he tried explaining the mechanics behind it. His plan was to be gone a week, maybe two depending on if he could help them with any reconstruction efforts. They had been at it for months by now, but rebuilding a town took years. A shaman with the goddess's authority could shave that time down considerably.

By the second week of his absence, the autumn leaves on the White Cliffs had all turned brown and begun to fall. I trained as much as I could as both a slinger and a newfound shaman, but I could only do so much of either. I had a near-impeachable reserve of stamina with the goddess's blessing, even if I did not understand how. This meant I could sling all day and not get tired—sweaty, but not tired. I did get bored, though, and then I would begin to worry about Denali. I would then turn to practicing the fundamentals of shamanic authority, most of which involved conversing with rocks and plants. Rocks were stubborn, and plants were willful, so the conversations were quite dull. In the end I spent the last week wandering the White Cliffs and talking with strangers, hopeful that I would run into Tokala and be able to check on her. Some of the shamans I ran into were keener for conversation than others. It was not until the end of the second week that I encountered our dinner friends, Beben and Kalaku.

"Amarantha, so good to see you," the couple said in unison as they beamed at me.

"I would have visited, but I didn't know how to find you," I replied.

"Where is Denali?" Beben asked.

"He made a quick journey to Roca for me. He should be back any day."

Our conversation was interrupted as Tokala walked by. Her eyes were noticeably darker, and her hair looked rather unkempt and greasy.

"Tokala!" I said in both shock and relief. "Will you join us?" I proffered.

"We hope to see you tonight," Kalaku said to Tokala.

Tokala paused for a moment. She did not offer anything beyond a slight wave of her hand and continued her shuffle. I knew how loneliness could affect people, but this seemed different, like she had not been sleeping. There was a sleep aid I could give her later if I could catch her again.

I turned back to Beben and Kalaku. "Should we follow her?"

"Oh no, dear. Best to give her some space right now. She's just been having a rough go. We've been dining with her every few days, but you, dear, you must be beside yourself. Let's check on Denali first. We'll see Tokala tonight."

The wandering daze I had been in for the last week cleared immediately.

"How will you get to him?" I asked, feeling my excitement rise.

"Oh, we don't leave the White Cliffs, dear. What good is longevity if you die from a stray orb?" Beben chuckled. "Let's head to the top of the cliffs. My equipment is up there."

The pair began walking in the wrong direction.

"There is a closer set of stairs this way," I said.

Kalaku turned and smiled. "Walking is good for the heart, and exercise has its place, but in the afternoon I don't like working up a sweat. We'll take the lift."

My perplexed look probably stayed on my face the whole time until it was swapped for bewilderment and then excitement.

"This basket will take us all the way up?" I asked.

"Very nearly." Beben smiled. "It's rudimentary, but it's all I could get approved for use at the White Cliffs. Some people here are vehemently opposed to technology, but they have a hard time deciding on where to draw the line. Apparently, pulleys and counterweights are acceptable."

"You two are my favorite people here," I said and genuinely meant it.

"Thank you," they said in unison again.

"You'll need to visit our laboratory in the valley sometime," Beben said.

"What is a laboratory?"

Kalaku squealed a little. "You'll love it. It's where we test any hypotheses we have." She paused as she saw the look on my face. "Um, where we practice new things and find better ways of doing them."

"Innovation!" I exclaimed.

"Exactly!" Kalaku bounced a little as she said it.

"Denali and I were just lamenting before he left that no one here seems to innovate in what's possible."

"We didn't want to bombard you two at dinner. Most find us too quirky to maintain our company," Kalaku said.

"Then it sounds like the company here at the White Cliffs has run stale. People need to get out more," I said.

"Indeed!" Beben exclaimed. "How many of them can look across the Unkubernan? We've a universe of possibilities to explore!" The basket lurched to a stop. "Ah, here we are. Follow me."

We climbed a few paces until we were at what seemed to be the highest vantage point of the White Cliffs.

"Now give me a moment, and I'll get it all set up."

I turned to Kalaku. "Is that a telescope?"

"Indeed. Have you never seen one? We use this one for stargazing."

"I've never seen one so large. Can I use that to see Roca?"

"Perhaps, but your angle would be limited; the curvature of the planet sees to that. What Beben is preparing is very similar in concept."

"Here we are." Beben pulled out a large curved reflective plate with string tied around it to a center package.

"What is it?" I asked.

"A totem I developed." He grinned. "If you don't mind, my dear."

"Of course," Kalaku said.

She approached him and cupped her hands around the reflective plate. I felt air begin to swirl around us.

"There we are," Kalaku said. "Now there is a pocket of air attached to the top of the plate. Beben will sling the plate out over the town, the shoot will deploy, and my pocket of air will maintain its lift. Along with a few other principles given the shape of the totem, well, we can explain the principles later. Here we go!"

Beben began swirling his hand back and forth to wind up his connection to the plate, then in one massive move he swung in a full circle and sent the plate flying into the Unkubernan. Kalaku reached forward and began swirling the air in front of us until crystals began to form.

"You're making a telescope," I said in awe.

"She has a special connection to air and water, a very rare affinity," Beben explained.

"I'm struggling with divination on rocks. I can't imagine speaking to air."

"You don't know until you try. Maybe you'll have a knack for it as well," Beben said with a smile.

The image before us was tracking the plate so that we could see the reflection. As it came upon the village, Beben stopped the plate. It shook for a moment, but the pocket of air must have successfully filled the shoot. The image steadied, and I saw the horrors in clear detail.

Beben and Kalaku both began moving their hands as they repositioned and focused on certain targets. They scanned what should have been a town to find that it was actually a small fort holding out against an army. Orbs were flying against stone ramparts, and flames burst in various locations. There were both shamans and slingers attacking in unison.

They focused in on the top of someone's head. It was Denali. My heart skipped to see he was still alive. He was behind a stone wall of the fort signaling others to move in various directions. The general was at work. He looked up and shaded his eyes to focus in on the plate. He smiled when he saw it and began to mouth something. He mouthed it slowly three times and got back to work.

"What is he saying? I can't hear!" My voice came out as a croak.

"I can read his lips," Kalaku said. "He says he will be running late, but they are fine."

"Fine? How can they be fine? He's fighting an army of shamans and slingers. He just doesn't want me to come. We need to go to him. He needs reinforcements."

The image faded as Beben and Kalaku turned to me.

"We're not warriors," they said hesitantly in unison.

"Then let's get others. How do I rally the other children? Can we go to the goddess?"

Beben and Kalaku shared a look that was interrupted by an explosion. A body hurdled over the cliffs. I ran to the edge, looking down at the chasm maze, and watched the figure twist until an explosion of red dirt and white rock blew around it, but it did not stop. From there it was propelled forward, this time of its own volition. It moved at a dizzying speed, leaving a trail of dust behind it. A massive black boulder followed behind the trail of dust.

Seattle was free.

CHAPTER 29

RALLYING CRY

I did not take the lift back down. I leapt down the stairs at unsafe speeds, even tumbling down the last few steps here and there. Crowds were moving to where Seattle had been quarantined for months as the corruption in his soul was studied and contained. I pushed through the throngs until I found Tokala's corpse in the corner of the room near Seattle's quarantine cell. Rochelle was examining the corpse.

"How did he escape?" I demanded.

Rochelle straightened and turned to address the crowd without looking at me directly.

"He did not escape. The goddess banished him for the murder of Tokala. Her single rule is absolute."

"That's an escape. He played you and the goddess."

Rochelle whipped an orb forward with enough force to attempt a humiliating smack across the cheek. I caught the orb in my hand instead. She yanked it back, dragging me forward. I did not let go until we were face-to-face.

"Try that again, Rochelle. I'm more than willing to be banished from this place." The stern woman scowled with flushed cheeks. I turned my back to her and addressed the crowd myself. "Listen up. There is a battle waging in the Unkubernan. Seattle's escape is no coincidence. Denali is holding off a small army of slingers and shamans in Roca. We need to save those people. We can put an end to a few gangs and remind the other gods that they have no jurisdiction in the Unkubernan."

A man from the crowd spoke up. "Let them have jurisdiction. There are no slingers of Roche left."

"Just because bonds are broken doesn't mean you should forsake your oaths," I said.

Rochelle stepped forward until we were shoulder to shoulder, but she did not look my way.

"Nobody here swore their oaths on Death as you and your reimagined order did. Anyone here who served under the original order of Roche fulfilled their oaths in their lifetime. They are forsaking nothing."

"So nobody here will help? What about Seattle's corruption? Are you willing to let that loose?"

"The goddess will notify the other gods, and they will hold council," Rochelle explained.

I scoffed. "The other gods won't care if he never leaves the Unkubernan. We can deal with this here and now."

Nobody gave any sign they wanted to intervene. I saw Beben and Kalaku attempting to enter the crowd to no avail, but they had already made their stance on the matter clear.

"Will none of you help? Even from a distance?" I pleaded.

Rochelle spoke up again to address the crowd. "We will hold a funeral for our departed sister. A vigil in her memory."

I slammed one of my orbs into the ground, cracking the stone floor. "A woman few of you bothered to help. She was clearly struggling." I glared out into the crowd, but no eyes met my gaze.

"In hindsight, it would seem Seattle was influencing her from afar, an advantage of the union I did not realize he had begun to tap into. We will lay our sister to rest," Rochelle said.

I turned and pointed a finger nearly at Rochelle's face. "You knew this was possible?"

Rochelle jumped back and put her hand to her hip. My threat before had clearly rattled her. I put my finger down and turned back to the crowd.

"Fine. You cowards hold a funeral and pretend you cared about Tokala while I go try to save another child of Ukaleq you lot don't seem interested in protecting. Don't bother fetching our corpses for a feigned care at a funeral."

I stormed through the crowd and made my way to my rooms to change into more rugged clothing and grab the travel pack I always kept at the ready.

CHAPTER 30

FRUITS OF LABOR

I descended the stairs of the White Cliffs with my six orbs, two waterskins, and a pack of fruit and dried meat. I wore the same clothes I had arrived at the White Cliffs in. I had since laundered Denali's blood out of them and patched them. It felt good to be in britches and boots again instead of those robes.

As I neared the base of the stairs, I caught the faintest smell of charcoal from a fire that had been burning continuously for a long time. I moved instinctively, thrusting myself into the air with my orbs in the same fashion Denali had told me was impossible. I could not sustain myself in the air, but I could use the force of my orbs to slow my descent and avoid breaking any bones upon my landing.

Two stones the size of my head ricocheted through the wall of the White Cliffs where I had just been. As I landed, I counted three slingers, including Samma, the small skinny one who had tried taking my face off. The second slinger, a massive man with broad shoulders, recalled his stones from the staircase. The third was massive in the waist, and his tricks were not yet obvious.

The best defense against three opponents was offense. I quickly dropped into the sixth Noble Form with all six of my orbs, nothing left in reserve. My feet moved like lightning as I surged forward. My orbs moved faster than I could see, but with three opponents, I could not fight by sight alone.

Samma deflected two of my orbs with ease. The broad-shouldered man barely blocked in time, but my orbs struck the third man in the heart, or so it had seemed. I heard the shattering of orbs instead of the piercing of flesh.

The third man ripped off his shirt in glee, exposing a torso covered in defensive orbs as orbs began to cover his head like a helmet. He let out a booming chuckle as I dodged a stone from the broad-shouldered man and deflected two impossibly fast orbs from Samma.

In response, I struck the fat man in the forehead before his orbs could finish covering him completely. I sent a second orb toward the broad-shouldered man before he could recall his stone to defend. These two were using cheap tricks that were only effective with backup or against inexperienced slingers. The two men fell dead. Samma was another matter.

I slipped into the third Noble Form and left two of my orbs in defensive positions. I struck forward with four of my orbs, just as I had when sparring with Rochelle so many months ago. I made sure not to be too linear this time. I was tempted to try the sixteenth Noble Form, as I had against Rochelle, but I could not risk it—not with how fast Samma was.

He had only displayed two orbs so far, and they were enough to keep up with my four orbs. He could still have some in reserve, just waiting for an opening. I swapped to the twelfth Noble Form and increased my velocity with wider arcs. It exposed me briefly, but it was a test to see if he would pull out another orb, which he did not. I could risk the fastest form, the sixteenth, but only because Samma was limited to two orbs. It was the only way to match his speed.

I nearly tripped to stop my orbs in time as Brule slammed down and devoured Samma in a massive crunch. He gobbled up the other two corpses as I recalled my orbs and caught my breath.

"Thank you, Brule."

He turned and hissed ferociously. I stepped backward, and his eyes softened.

"Amarantha," he said. "I apologize. My nature was catching up to me. It is I who must be thanking you. These three have been hunting me since they arrived. I am finally rid of them thanks to you."

"I'm happy to help. I wish I could stay and chat, but I'm in a hurry." I turned to leave as the rest of the words spilled out in a jumble. "Denali is fighting a battle against shamans and slingers. You probably saw Seattle's escape from down here. I have to go help Denali."

"Wait," the massive demigod hissed.

I stopped as I realized I had no idea which portal would take me out and which would leave me stuck in the labyrinth. I turned to face Brule.

"Over here. Did the other Children of Ukaleq not tell you?"

"Tell me what?" I asked as I followed.

"There are portals to each of the settlements originally established by the shamans. Take this one."

I stared at the steep wall of the White Cliffs. "This would have been helpful information. Is it one-way like in the labyrinth?"

"No. Are you going alone?" he said as he coiled himself behind me.

"Nobody was willing to help or even offer guidance, I suppose. It seems Seattle didn't know about these either," I said.

"They are not a practical bunch. Not anymore."

"Thank you, Brule. I may be sending refugees through. Please don't eat them."

The demigod buried himself in his coil. "I'm quite full now."

I stepped through the wall and emerged on a plateau outside of Roca.

CHAPTER 31

SAFETY

I used my vantage on the plateau to gauge the status of the siege. It was far too quiet. There did not seem to be any movement on any of the fronts outside of town.

I descended the plateau and hurried toward the town as quickly as I dared without exposing myself to the enemy. As I neared and saw the situation, I picked up speed. I ran by corpse after corpse in the hard dry dirt.

It was a gruesome scene. Bodies with holes the size of a fist lay in puddles of dry blood. Charred remains still let off their putrid smell. Shamans and slingers alike were strewn about, hundreds of them.

As I neared the town, I found myself screaming, “Denali!”

A figure popped out over one of the solid stone walls. When had stone walls been erected? The figure dropped down and began dashing for me.

“Amarantha!”

We sprinted into each other and collapsed to our knees in a tight embrace on the battlefield.

“What happened?” I said as I clung to him, squeezing and touching so fiercely that I worried I might hurt him.

“I have never commanded so much authority before. I thought I might burn out.” He wheezed a few breaths. “Sorry, I am quite tired, as you can imagine.”

I laughed and wiped away some of my tears. “I can imagine. How did you do it?”

“I erected the walls from the earth to protect from Seattle’s slingers. They started showing up the same time I did. Kilo and I were handling them strategically.”

“Kilo? The kid they replaced me with?” I interrupted.

“Aye, we picked them off one at a time without putting any risk on ourselves. It got a little dicey when the shamans started showing up. They were more powerful than they should have been. It took me a few days to realize that Pahokute had erected his own totem out here. Back when you said you’d faced him possessing the shaman, he was establishing his authority here in the Unkubernan. I destroyed the totem he had erected with flames, and all the shamans who had been drawing authority from it burst into flames. I have never seen anything like it.” He gestured to the burnt corpses surrounding us. “It felt like a war crime, honestly. Not sure I would have done it if I had known. Then again, raiding a village to get to one man feels like a war crime on their part. I'm rambling. I'm tired." He smiled weakly.

I helped him to his feet. "We're not out of the woods yet. Seattle escaped."

"Oh, gods. Is he coming? I am too tired to face him right now, Amarantha. If I command much more authority, I will pass out."

"He was heading to his fort at a rapid speed. I don't know when he'll realize the action is out here or how long we have. We need to evacuate before it's too late. See that plateau?"

He raised a hand to his eyes for shade as he peered into the distance. "That one?"

I closed my eyes and summoned my massive boulder so it floated over the location of the portal. I opened my eyes in time to see his eyes grow wide and his weak smile grow into a broad grin.

"Amazing," he said.

I grinned at hearing the pride in his voice. "Head there, and I'll get the villagers. Do they have any wounded?"

"No." He shook his head and then blinked a few times at the rapid movement.

"Fantastic. We'll be right behind you. Take this waterskin." I pushed the skin into his hands.

His face was pale from exhaustion, and his eyes were heavy. He began walking slowly toward the plateau while I left to fetch the rest of the town.

CHAPTER 32

SHOWDOWN

The sun was already getting low. I sat at the ridge of the plateau and used my boulder with a rope tied to it as a counterweight like Beben and Kalaku had shown me. My eyes stayed focused on the horizon, searching for any sign of Seattle. There were no elderly—beside the old invoker, Tali—to evacuate, and there was only a handful of small children, but the people were tired from weeks of siege. I did not have the heart to warn them about the stairs required to ascend the White Cliffs.

Dalek and two of the other council members led the group with the children first and ushered everyone through what appeared to them to be a flat stone wall. I could see Monte and Dayani taking up the rear. I had not had the chance to address them when I started the evacuation. There was too much work to be done getting everyone mobile.

There were faces in the stream of people I did not recognize. This realization filled me with guilt until Denali explained that more people had joined the caravan from Takan to help with the rebuilding efforts in Roca. My guilt shifted to a quiet sense of hope. It came as quite a surprise that anyone would want to help rebuild a broken town or risk the wrath of a gang like the Kingmakers. Apparently, reassurance that the last true slinger of Roche was taking care of the threat was enough to convince them to uproot. Their options must have been pretty bleak in Takan.

Denali came and sat down beside me.

"Do you need a break?" he asked.

"Hmm? Oh, no. It's not taking much effort to move the boulder."

"I cannot stop watching it move. It seems so unreal," he said.

"It's how Seattle fights."

"Hmm." Denali's baritone hummed as he contemplated the potential battle with a boulder that seemingly defied gravity and moved freely. "So, what signs are we watching for on the horizon?"

"Dust clouds. When he took off from the White Cliffs, he moved at an alarming rate and drove up clouds of dust behind him," I explained.

We sat in silence for a few minutes. My attention was split between using my boulder as a counterweight, scanning the horizon, and listening to Denali breathe. He was so tired, it almost sounded like when he was deep asleep. As peaceful as it was, my mind still raced.

I finally interrupted the quiet. "I might not get another chance like this to take him down. Maybe we should be laying a trap for him."

Denali shook his head. "No, Amarantha. If we need to face him, we do it together. Now is not the time."

"I can't help but feel responsible for any damage he does while on the loose. It was my charge to bring him to justice. The people of the Unkubernan know that now. They'll lose faith in the slingers of Roche all over again. Even if there aren't any left right now, there could be someday. I don't want the reputation dying with me."

No one climbed onto the rope as I waited with my boulder. I looked around just as Monte placed a hand on my shoulder.

"Thank you, Amarantha," he said.

"Is that everyone?" I asked.

Monte and Dayani were the only people left on the plateau besides me and Denali. I climbed to my feet, and Monte pulled me into a tight hug. Dayani ran forward and joined the embrace.

"We are so proud of you," Monte said as Dayani sniffled, holding back a few tears. "Let's go. I have written two more sonnets since you promised to listen to the last one."

Something in the air changed. I did not know if it was the smell of rain, the crackle in the air that made my hair stand on end, or the deep roar of something moving faster than it should, but it happened all at once. I pushed Monte and Dayani as hard as I could, and they tumbled backward into the portal. My boulder was overhead, but it was not enough to stop the pressure pushing down on it entirely.

Denali's staff was pushing up against my boulder as well. Denali grabbed me and pulled me off the edge of the plateau as my boulder crashed down into where we had been standing.

Seattle shot out of the dust cloud that erupted above, his long black hair streaming behind him in greasy strands. I looked over to Denali next to me as the cushion of air he had summoned vanished, and we dropped a few inches to the ground.

"Hide," I hissed at him.

He nodded as he coughed and crawled away to hide behind some of the rubble. His staff was nowhere to be seen. As untrained as he was at slinging, he may even have been too tired to sling it back to himself.

I ran toward Seattle, putting as much distance as possible between myself and Denali in his compromised state. Seattle's back was to me as he surveyed the town and the corpses that littered the surrounding area. I was not going to wait for any exchange of words or philosophies. I needed this man dead, and there was more than enough proof of truth to warrant it, even if it meant I would never enter the White Cliffs again. This was my sworn duty.

I slung two of my orbs forward faster than I had realized I could. They closed the distance between us so quickly that I heard a small clap in the air. I immediately realized that I was not just slinging them; I was pouring my emotion and my desire into my authority over them, just as I had done to move the boulder.

Despite the speed, they ricocheted away from Seattle before they could pierce his flesh. He did not even turn around. I launched multiple attacks with the two orbs, each faster than the last, but nothing broke his defense. I began to scream as I ran toward him, frustrated that I could not close the distance more quickly.

I dropped two orbs to my heels and used them to propel myself forward. My stride wobbled at first, but I quickly found myself gliding at ridiculous speeds toward Seattle. The claps resounding in the air from my two orbs continued, but nothing worked. My boulder flew overhead, moving faster than I could propel myself without falling flat on my face.

Everything froze for a moment as Seattle's boulder appeared over his head, blocking my own from smashing him. Then came a sudden deep clap that reverberated through my bones, as though the sound had to catch up to what I was witnessing. I slowly, and not very gracefully, came to a stop and blinked a few times.

Seattle's feet floated off the ground, and he slowly turned toward me. I recalled my two offensive orbs and my boulder. I dropped into the second Noble Form but allowed my orbs and my boulder to encircle me freely without even slinging them in the traditional sense. My totems knew the dance as well as I did.

I hesitantly balanced myself in the second stance on the orb under each heel and ascended from the ground, matching Seattle's tactics.

"You truly are Slalal's brat. You've become quite the thorn in my side," he bellowed as he slowly closed the distance between us.

I could tell from his posture alone that I was outclassed. Even if I could do all the things he could, he had centuries more practice. My sparring session with Rochelle, the originator of the slingers and the Noble Forms, had given me too much confidence in my abilities.

My realization was enough of a slip in my focus to present an opening for Seattle. He gave no physical sign of his intention, and there was no possibility of seeing or hearing his orb before it could strike. My mental awareness of the fight was just fast enough for me to deflect his orb into piercing my shoulder instead of my heart, and the orb ripped out through the muscle in my shoulder. My eyes opened wide, and sweat began to pool into drips on my forehead as the consequences of fighting at this level played out in my mind.

"That's right," he said. "I could have changed orientation at that speed and still pierced your heart, but I'd like to have a chat first."

I could not respond. My breathing turned to heaves, and my mind looped in panic.

How do I stop an orb that defies the laws of nature? It can move at any speed, it can change any direction without losing speed, it can only be stopped by my own orbs, and to what effect? To spin the other direction as soon as it has been stopped? My orbs cannot hold his orbs, can they? My breathing began to slow, and my eyes began to take in my surroundings again.

"There she is," Seattle said with a wicked grin.

I stared him down to give him the audience he was patiently waiting for, but I got to work on the shaman training Denali had been teaching me. I slowly began changing the shape of my six orbs and my boulder without drawing attention from Seattle. They would no longer fly through the air without resistance, but with my new techniques the wind did not impact the speed anyhow.

"Now that you've had time to see how worthless the children and the goddess are, you agree with me, don't you? I heard every conversation you had with Tokala."

I continued to stare in his direction as I slowly worked my totems, but I gave him no response.

"Clearly, we both want the same thing. We want to bring order to the Unkubernan. That was the whole reason Slalal and I reformed the Roche slingers in the first place. Just because the gods have abandoned us doesn't mean we shouldn't be able to live in harmony and prosper."

"We don't need gods out here," I said.

"No, but we need a leader. A united banner. Not like the noble slingers of Roche, though. What good is a group that brings justice and upholds law and order if there is no executive leader to declare what laws are fair? We need a king, and a king needs an enforcer." He gestured to me.

I could not help but laugh. "You should have stayed with the goddess until she could fix whatever is happening to your blackened soul. The people of the Unkubernan won't subjugate themselves to a king. If they wanted that, then they would have left for the coast to live under the jurisdiction of a great spirit. You'll kill all who refuse you and find yourself to be a king with no subjects."

Seattle chuckled. "Why do you think Slalal and I collected children?"

"Slalal rescued children," I clarified.

"Not at first." There was a sneer on his face that resonated in his tone. "More than a century ago, our goal was to build a kingdom with a new generation, but my brother fell in love with the creed written in Roche and made everyone swear to the ideals."

I had heard enough, and my totems were ready. I dropped to the ground and slung all six of my orbs forward. Each orb had expanded and was now shaped with a cavity. As Seattle used his three orbs to block mine, I snatched them and trapped them inside my own. He dropped to the ground as his remaining two orbs left his heels and flew to block my orbs, but their interception resulted in their capture. My sixth and final orb struck him in the gut. He slung his boulder forward, but my boulder was able to stop his. The cavity in my boulder was not deep enough to trap his boulder, but it was enough to act as a shield that I could balance against his attack.

He began to laugh as he clutched his stomach. "Well played, but what about the hostage?"

"Hostage?" My whole jaw quivered as the words left my lips.

I turned to look back toward Denali. He was distant, but I could make out a splash of red followed by his figure falling to the ground.

My vision turned white as I screamed. I could feel Seattle's orbs fighting to gain their freedom from my own. His massive boulder swirled, attempting to get around mine, and pounded against it when it could not. I sent my only remaining orb, the one that had pierced his gut, toward his head. I wanted his head.

My vision returned from the white-hot rage as I expected to find Seattle's head with a hole in it, but I was too late. His final orb, which he had just used to hurt Denali, was blocking my final shot. We were matched. My six orbs encased his, but we wrestled for control. Even our boulders wrestled. Neither of us could strike the other, but I needed him dead. I needed to help Denali.

I looked to Seattle and saw my orb only a few inches from piercing him. Pushing against his orb was a matter of will. I could still kill him if I could get it to move a few inches. His smile drew into a wicked grin as his eyes changed focus from me to the orb hovering in front of him. My eyes focused to see Denali's blood dripping from his encased orb.

Everything became red. At first I thought my vision was changing again in my rage, but I could still see Seattle. His wicked grin faded as he bared his teeth, his nostrils flared. He let out a guttural roar as he spread his feet to widen his stance. My vision was fine; it was my orbs turning red. They burned like the sun until they turned white. Seattle's boulder began to melt and drip to the ground. The other six orbs also dripped white until there was nothing holding my orbs back anymore. I pushed through with all my rage and skewered Seattle with all six orbs. What was left of his boulder crashed to the ground as he did.

There was no time to savor my victory. I jumped onto my boulder and rode it back toward Denali as quickly as I could without being blown off of it. The wind blared in my ears until I could hear nothing but my own frantic thoughts.

I jumped down beside him and scooped him into my lap. His eyes were open. His chest was heaving. He looked to me and tried to mouth something, but he coughed up blood instead. I ripped off his shirt to see the holes that riddled his chest and his neck. Some were healed, but some were not closing properly. He was too weak. It was not a lack of power—the goddess provided enough of that. He just did not have the strength left, and I did not have the training to heal him myself.

My eyes darted all over his wounds and his expression for any sign of how to help. I could stop the bleeding in some areas, but some of these should have been fatal. He was not looking at me; he kept looking to his left. I scanned the area and saw his totem. I reached and grabbed the staff to put it in his hands. The hole near his heart immediately closed up, but he was still struggling to breathe and close the holes in his neck. The blood began to slow, but the wounds did not appear to be closing.

His eyes were distant. Before I realized what was happening, his staff shot from his hand like a spear, followed by the sound of skewered flesh and more coughed blood.

I turned to see Seattle with Denali's staff through his heart. When I turned to look back to Denali, his eyes were shut and his breathing had stopped. He was gone.

GOODBYE

I held Denali in my arms as we rode the boulder through the portal and ascended the White Cliffs. I did not look at anyone as we came through, and their voices were drowned out as the wind whipped in my ears. The only light came from the night sky reflecting off the pure white of the cliffs.

We, I thought to myself. I held his body, but I knew it was not him. Not anymore. His thick chest lay bare in my lap. It was the same hairy military chest I had pressed up against for months now. His hair still smelled deeply of his sweat, a smell I had oddly grown to enjoy, but none of it was truly him anymore.

I looked to my shoulder where I sensed a touch but saw nothing. I could feel his hand there. His spirit would not stay long. We flew up and over the White Cliffs. Some of the refugees had already crested the stairs and were gathering in the illuminated stone garden as the Children of Ukaleq gathered to see the commotion. They all looked up as I flew overhead.

I descended into the courtyard where the goddess had sealed me and Denali together for eternity.

"Ukaleq!" I pleaded. "Is there nothing you can do?"

The emotions hit me at once as I spoke, and I began to sob. I pulled Denali's body closer and stood on shaky legs so that I could get down from the boulder. I laid him down in the grass before the goddess's statue and caressed my tears away from his cheek.

I watched my body fall over Denali's and saw my own luminous form as I was pulled into the spiritual realm. I was getting used to this, but the fact that Denali's luminous form was not near his body shocked me. The goddess stood before me. Her patterns swirled, but in my grief my mind did not wander into the complexity of her patterns.

"All I can give you is a chance to say goodbye, my child."

"Thank you," I said, expecting my voice to waver, but there was no body associated with the voice.

I turned to see Denali standing behind me. His hand was on my shoulder just as I had felt, but even as luminous beings, our touch did not have the same effect as before. I clasped on to him, hoping for the deep connection we had felt together last time, but I could not touch him like that anymore.

"You're different now," I said.

"Apologies," he said as he nodded. "I do not have much time."

"Is there a reaper?" I asked as I looked around.

"No, reapers are quite rare and usually . . ." The luminous patterns of his face showed a smile. "There is so much I wanted to explore with you. I wanted to see the world through your eyes."

"Can you stay with me?" I asked.

"No. There is a natural order to things. I do not understand it, but I can feel it."

"I'm not ready to be alone again," I said.

"We are partners for eternity, remember? I will be back. You will find me."

I put my hand to the patterns on his cheek and followed them down to his chest.

"I will find you, Denali. I love you."

"And I love you, Amarantha." His form began to fade. The patterns were trailing off into the distance. They were going somewhere. "Do me one favor. Live your life outside of the Unkubernan. See the world. Live up to your potential. Do not hide yourself away again. This world needs you. I can feel it to be true. Goodbye for now, my love."

I watched the trail of his patterns leave up into the starry sky.

CHAPTER 34

OATHS

I did not open my eyes right away. Even as the sound of murmuring filled the courtyard, I kept my eyes closed and held Denali's body in my arms.

"Clear a path," a familiar voice boomed over the murmuring. "What is the meaning of this? Who are all these people?"

I opened my eyes to see Rochelle burst through a portion of the crowd. She stopped abruptly at the sight of Denali's corpse.

The illumination from the stones in the courtyard grew dark as the goddess drew in light to appear before us.

"Goddess, who are all these people? What has happened?" Rochelle asked with her head bowed as she approached.

"These children are refugees," the goddess said.

"They cannot stay; they have not earned the privilege," Rochelle argued.

"All who come before me are welcome to my blessing if they join in union," the goddess explained without emotion.

"That would be chaos, Your Grace. That is why we instituted the maze."

"That would be why the world knows my children as chaotics. There is balance in all things." Rochelle's face turned sour at the expression as the goddess continued. "I have instituted no such obstacles to those in search of my blessing. My word is that all who come before me must receive my blessing in union and never slay another child of mine or face banishment. That is all."

The goddess's figure began to fade, and the light returned to the stones around us.

"It is a privilege to be here!" Rochelle yelled for everyone to hear. "I am the founder of Roche. I built the slingers of Roche when the gods abandoned us. I and the other children have spent lifetimes of service to achieve the utopia we have cultivated here."

"Are you going to play gatekeeper?" I asked as I laid Denali's body down gently from my lap. "Tell me, Rochelle, when was the last time you spent a lifetime in service to anyone beside yourself or your own ego?" I rose to my feet and marched toward her. "Ten thousand years ago? More?"

"Watch your insolent tone, child," the woman hissed.

"Do you really want to push me right now?" I gestured to Denali's corpse. "My threat from before is even stronger. I'll take a banishment if I need to deal with you."

Rochelle stepped forward menacingly but stopped short of attacking me.

"But you won't risk banishment, will you?" I said as I cocked my head. "In fact, I'm willing to bet on it."

I walked over to Ukaleq's statue and placed my right hand on it.

"What are you doing?" Rochelle asked as she clutched her stomach.

"I swear my life, upon the goddess Ukaleq, that if Rochelle does not purpose her life to the very oaths she wrote, then my life is Ukaleq's."

The statue glowed, and the swear was sealed. Rochelle fell to her knees.

"What have you done?"

I walked over to her so she could look up at me as I spoke. "You are going to walk the walk for the people of the Unkubernan. You're going to build up the slingers of Roche one more time. If you don't, then I die, which will be blood on your hands. That means you will be banished from the White Cliffs forever, banished from your utopia. I'll be back in a lifetime or two to check on you. If you've been good, I may even ask the goddess to break the bond. Something to look forward to."

I walked over to Denali's body and hoisted it onto my boulder. When I caught sight of Beben and Kalaku in the crowd, I walked toward them with my boulder in tow. I left Rochelle's wails and moans behind me.

"Let's head back to your chambers. We can consecrate Denali and preserve him in stone," Beben explained as we left the increasingly crowded square.

"What have you sealed upon yourself?" Kalaku asked in a hushed tone. "How did you get the goddess to agree to that pledge and seal it? Her rule about killing one of her children is absolute. She cannot take your life."

"Oaths are up to interpretation," I explained. "I only swore my life to Ukaleq, I did not say she had to kill me. The goddess understood the distinction. We'll see how long it takes Rochelle to figure it out. She'll do some good in the meantime, maybe remember what it means to be human."

CHAPTER 35

GRIEF

At some point during the night I fell asleep on the bench near Denali's remains. Beben and Kalaku had encased his body in stone, or turned his flesh to stone; I honestly was not sure how they had done it. I pushed myself up against the stiffness in both my neck and my back and looked to Denali's stone face. He looked so peaceful, so exquisite, so real. Even though I knew he was gone, I could not stop staring. I worried I might forget what he looked like if I did.

I looked over and saw Monte and Dayani standing in the open doorway. None of the Children of Ukaleq had entered throughout the night. The late evening had turned to an unannounced vigil. Those of Ukaleq's children who came by chose to pay their respects from the hall. Only the people of Roca had come in to say goodbye to the general who had saved them. I did not remember who came or what they had said. Dalek had come with his boys. He was wearing the official beads of the chief when he came, an indication that he had finally accepted the position formally. The boys had not said a word; they simply held each of my hands for a while and cried with me. They had seen too much death already and had grieved more than any child should have to.

It had been a long night, but the sun was rising now, and Monte and Dayani waited to enter. I nodded for them to come in. They walked reverently into the stone courtyard and sat down beside me on my makeshift bed. None of us said anything for a long while. We just sat in the early morning light that peeked in from the south-facing veranda. The dry dead leaves of the autumn season littered the stone floor and blew around our ankles, but new shoots were already sprouting in the trees.

"Will you stay?" Dayani asked, breaking the silence.

"No," I responded slowly.

"What will you do?" Monte asked.

I thought for a long while before I answered.

"I swore my oaths as a slinger of Roche when I lost everyone and everything. I knew I would be the last, that I would be alone, but I did it anyway. And then I hid behind the sudden responsibility in Roca. My mentor always told me that walking a noble path, following the covenant, meant sacrifice, and sometimes that meant being alone. I've been telling myself for so long now that walking a noble path is something you do alone. And here I am, back where I started. Alone. But for a time I wasn't alone. And during that time, we dreamed together. There was a future that we could control. I don't know what that future is now. I was meant to spend it with him. I still can someday. I guess I'm not really alone, not anymore. I can feel him out there. I don't understand this connection, but I know I'll be with him again someday." I sighed deeply, and then I laughed at myself. "I'm not answering your question."

Monte wrapped his arm around me, and I started to cry again. I did not have many tears left, but my breathing was irregular as my body tried to cry anyway.

"Deep breaths, dear," Dayani said, placing her hand on my back.

Her hand helped, and my breathing returned to normal. Monte kept his arm around me, and Dayani left her hand on my back.

"I don't know how to grieve right now. I feel like I'm doing it all wrong. I was able to say goodbye, and I find peace knowing that I'll see him again, that I can feel him out there even now, but I hurt when he I look over and he isn't there."

"Maybe this will help." Monte handed me Denali's staff from under his cloak. "Beben fetched it for you. It's not Denali, but you should feel him when the moments are too much to bear."

I clasped the thick totem in my hands and felt a warm emotion of reassurance wash over me.

"There is so much I don't know about him, about our connection. I think I'll start there, to answer your question. Denali always said there was more to learn and explore out in the world than we'd find in the collected knowledge of hermits."

"It is a vast world for certain." Monte nodded to himself. "Dayani and I spent the better portion of our youth traveling the world before we made our way to the Unkubernan."

"Why stop? Why come to the Unkubernan?" I asked.

"We were no longer welcome by most great spirits, and we found the plight of others like ourselves. Refugees making the journey into the Unkubernan, not for a pilgrimage, but to escape the will and war of gods. To forge a new path."

"The pilgrimage did become a goal of ours," Dayani said. "But when we made it to Roca, we saw too many friends never return, so we lived on the edge of hope."

"And now you've made it." I smiled, then looked to Denali's stone face and remembered the happy months we had spent here. "Together."

Monte pulled his arm back and stood. "We will ask Ukaleq for her blessing, but we will follow your example. We will get back to work. The entire Unkubernan is suffering."

"It's safer here. You've earned your respite," I said.

Monte chuckled. "Believe it or not, there are more chaotics—more, um, Children of Ukaleq—out in the world than there are here in the White Cliffs. It takes a special kind of person to sit still for thousands of years and hoard resources."

Beben and Kalaku walked into the courtyard and cleared their throats in unison to make their presence known. Monte's words about hoarding resources, refugees, and the pilgrimage played in my mind. I stood and walked over to the map, leaving Denali's side for the first time.

"I fear I've put you all in more danger," I said as they joined me around the map table Denali and I had daydreamed over for months. "I spoke of only one side of the coin when I, for a lack of a better term, cursed Rochelle."

They followed my fingers as I traced the borders of the Unkubernan and counted the number of bordering nations and then traced the pilgrimage paths that led from each nation toward Roca.

"I don't understand Ukaleq's willingness to let any who come before her as a couple receive her blessing. That is how we ended up with a creature like Seattle, and that is how we earned the term *chaotic*. I understand why Rochelle hid the White Cliffs behind a labyrinth and reserved it for esteemed shamans and those who retired from the order of Roche. It's worked for millennia. It would be nice to think that our people could maintain their independence and free will, but what about shamans from other nations? Would they come and receive the blessing to further their own god's will? Are some gates needed? Or would it all just turn into—"

"Chaos." Tali stood with the group around the table.

I was startled to see the old shit-fire invoker standing there.

"Don't trouble yourself over it, Amarantha. The Unkubernan and the White Cliffs will sort themselves out. There are better and more humane ways of rooting out the trash." He nodded to Beben and Kalaku.

"Yes, so good to see you again, Tali. It's been a long time," Kalaku said. "You are correct. After the incident with Seattle's corrupted soul, we could reenact the rites of invokers from long ago."

Questions sat on the tip of my tongue, ready to spill forth, but Tali pointed at me. "You don't need to concern yourself with it. It is our responsibility now. You are no longer Amarantha, the Last Slinger of Roche. You are Amarantha, the Chaotic. But you still have much to learn, and unfortunately, the answers to your immediate questions lie outside the White Cliffs."

Tali was different somehow. The air around him hummed, and he gave off a sense of authority I had never felt from him before. The bitter old man I had argued with for years suddenly seemed to be the only person in the world who knew what needed to happen next.

"What are you? Some kind of prophet?"

He folded his arms. "I told you as much. I'm an invoker."

Monte nodded in agreement.

"Which god do you speak for?" I asked.

"None." He spat on the floor, revealing some of his crass character again. "I watch the patterns of creation and sing their hymns. The great spirits of the world have not been acting in accordance with the creator for a very long time." He looked over his shoulder and up to the sky. "Except Her Grace Ukaleq, of course." He gave a slight bow as he kept his eyes trained on the sky as though lightning might come down and strike him. Everyone took a step back from him as they also examined the sky. He finally looked down and shook his head.

"I want to apologize, Amarantha. If I'd been acting as a true invoker all these years, then I would've seen your oaths. I was blinded by grief and disbelief while hiding under a rock of comfort in Roca. I want to make amends."

"How?" I asked.

He crossed his arms. "I don't want you to hide under the same dark cloud of grief I did. I know who you need to seek out. There is a chaotic known as Dutsi. He has a spiritual gift to see what others cannot. His gift may guide you to the answers you seek. Your connection with Denali is not unique among chaotics, but how it plays out in the reincarnation cycle is always unique, and Dutsi's gift can peer into the cycle. He can also help you find the source of the darkness in Seattle's spirit. The stories I have heard are most troubling. Even I do not have answers from the hymns of the creator. This is something new."

I walked over and held out a hand to shake his. "Thank you," I said, but he only stared at my outreached hand. "You old shit-fire," I added.

He smiled and clasped my hand. I pulled him in for a hug and felt the arms of Monte, Dayani, Beben, and Kalaku around me. Two pairs of shorter arms reached around my hips. I looked up to see Dalek standing in the doorway, smiling. His boys were holding me tight. I knew that Winona would be happy for her family because this was my family now, and I was happy for them.

Learn more about

Ryan Rhodes

RMRhodes.com

www.twitter.com/RockyRhyno

www.facebook.com/AuthorRMRhodes

www.youtube.com/channel/
UCNpdLbzWB9sgnz7O2qM3f4A

www.twitch.tv/AuthorRMRhodes

www.ingramcontent.com/pod-product-compliance
Lightning Source LLC
Chambersburg PA
CBHW020329030826
48979CB00021B/497

* 9 7 9 8 9 8 5 4 3 9 3 2 8 *